IRON BONES

BOOK 4

CRAIG HALLORAN

Dragon Wars: Iron Bones - Book 4

By Craig Halloran

★ ★ ★ ★

Dragon Wars is a registered trademark

Amazon Edition

TWO-TEN BOOK PRESS

PO Box 4215, Charleston, WV 25364

ISBN eBook: 978-1-946218-72-8

ISBN Paperback: 978-1-654648-88-6

ISBN Hardback: 978-1-946218-73-5

www.craighalloran.com

Publisher's Note

This book is a work of fiction. Names, characters, places, and incidents either are the product of the author's imagination or are used fictitiously, and any resemblance to actual persons, living or dead, events, or locales is entirely coincidental.

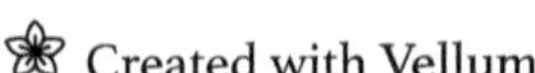 Created with Vellum

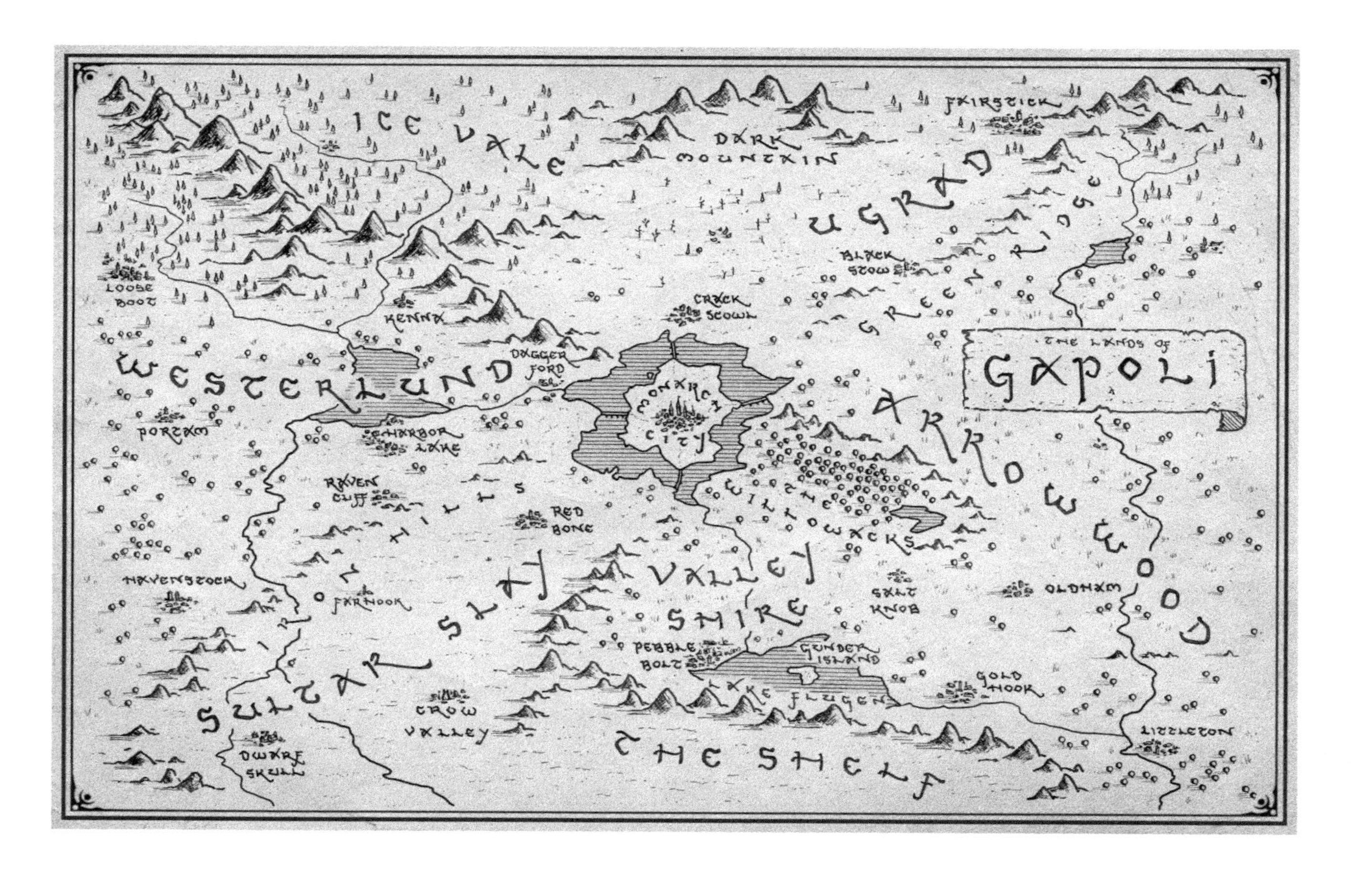

THE LANDS OF GAPOLI
ICE VALE
DARK MOUNTAIN
FAIRSTICK
UGRAD
GREEN RIDGE
BLACK SLOW
CRACK SCOWL
LOOSE BOOT
KENNA
WESTERLUND
DAGGER FORD
MONARCH CITY
ARROW WOOD
PORTAM
CHARBOR LAKE
RAVEN CLIFF
HILLS
RED BONE
WILLOWACKS
HAVENSTOCK
FARNOOK
SULTAR SLAY
VALLEY
SHIRE
SALT KNOB
OLDHAM
PEBBLE BOLT
GUNDER ISLAND
GOLD HOOK
LAKE FLUGEN
CROW VALLEY
DWARF SKULL
THE SHELF
LITTLETON

DARK MOUNTAIN

Outside of the Doom Riders' barracks, Iron Bones stood tall with his fists clenched at his sides and his blond hair hanging in his eyes. His family was watching from the retaining wall that surrounded the training facility. His mother, Drysis, was leaning against the wall. Her long white hair had many braids, and a black eye patch covered her left eye. She was wearing a suit of black leather armor. Her face remained as cold as stone.

"Iron Bones," Drysis said in her commanding voice. "Are you ready?"

Dyphestive nodded at her. "Always."

"I don't think he's ready," Scar said as he spit on the ground. He had a gravelly voice and a mean disposition, and his face had many red, irritated lacerations. He was dressed from the neck down in dark leather armor that looked like dragon scales. "Twenty silver chips say he takes a pummeling this time."

"I'll take that wager," Shamrok said with a nod. Sitting on the wall, he was dressed the same as Scar but had longer flame-red hair. His voice hinted at a much easier-going demeanor. He slapped a small sack on the wall, making the distinctive sound of jingling coins. "I believe in my brother."

"Huh, you're gonna lose," Scar said as he raked his fingers through his thick brown hair. He spit again.

That left one more Doom Rider standing along the wall —Ghost, who was dressed the same as his brothers, but he was wearing a dyed-blue leather skull-face mask. He never said a word.

Iron Bones didn't give any of his brothers a glance, even though he heard what they said. He was indifferent about it. He'd lost his memory when a gourn kicked him in the head, though he didn't even remember the incident. All he knew was what Drysis had told him. He was Iron Bones. They were his family. She was his mother, and they were his brothers. Nothing else mattered.

Drysis's gaze swung toward a covered wagon that had pulled up alongside the outside of the wall. A chisel-faced man in leather armor was standing at the back of the wagon, and a formidable-looking orc and a lizard man accompanied him. All of them were tall, muscular, sullen eyed, and ugly. "Who's first?" she asked.

The man started to open his mouth to speak, but the orc stepped in front of him and said, "I'll go." He had a wide face and flared nostrils, and his broad, muscular, hairy chest was bare. Cracking his neck, he faced off against Iron Bones and eyed him up and down. "He's barely a man. And you're paying me ten gold to fight him?"

Drysis nodded. "Twenty if you beat him."

The orc grunted. "I'll be glad to take your money." He balled up his fists, and his knuckles cracked. "Anything goes?"

"Of course," Shamrok said, "but remember, you don't get paid if you're dead."

Stiffening, the orc gave Iron Bones a cautious look for a moment and said, "It's not me that you should be worried about."

"Let's get on with it then." Shamrok hopped down from the wall and approached Iron Bones and the orc. "Anything goes. The fight doesn't stop until I say so. Clear?"

Iron Bones and the orc nodded.

Shamrok backed away and lifted then dropped his hands. "Fight!"

The orc's fist crashed into Iron Bones's jaw with jarring impact, and his head snapped to the side, but he brought his arms up in time to block the orc's next punch, which landed on his meaty forearms. A fierce uppercut rocked Iron Bones in the belly, and he doubled over.

"Fight back, brother!" Shamrok shouted.

Scar started laughing. "I told you he couldn't fight."

The orc's hard fists clobbered him all over. *Whap! Crack! Pop! Pop! Smack!*

Iron Bones took multiple shots to the chin, face, and gut. When he lowered his arms, he got popped in the face, and when he raised his fists, he took a shot in the belly. The orc was a brawler that was used to beating people to death. Iron Bones locked his arms around the orc and hung on for his life. But the orc body-slammed him to the ground.

"Oof!"

"Get up, you moron!" Shamrok shouted. "That ain't how we taught you to fight!"

The orc pressed his face into the ground and raked it over the gravel. He was as strong as a bull.

Iron Bones twisted out from underneath the orc and shoved the brute away. He scrambled back to his feet, panted, and wiped the blood from his lips.

"Look at him—he's cleaning himself like a cat. Sheesh!" Scar said.

The orc tossed his head back, flexed his arms, and let out a wild, triumphant yell.

After catching his breath, Iron Bones beckoned the orc forward with his heavy arms and big fists. He felt the biting sting of the orc's heavy fists, but that was it. His blood burned, a fire lit inside him.

The orc came at him and unloaded a flurry of hard punches. Iron Bones absorbed the blows with his body and his arms. A powerful jab slipped through and cracked him in the nose, and his eyes watered. He unleashed a haymaker of his own, but the orc ducked, and the punch swished over his head. Then the orc slipped behind him, grabbed him by the waist, and threw him to the ground.

They wrestled over the dusty ground in a tangle of brawny limbs. One rolled over the other, throwing rabbit punches and butting heads. The orc latched onto Iron Bones's neck and seized him in a fierce headlock. His eyes bulged, and his breath was cut short.

"What in the blazes are you *doing*, Iron Bones?" Shamrok shouted at the top of his lungs. "I've got money on this. Now start fighting like we taught you!"

Iron Bones's fingers clawed at the air, and his face turned red and purple.

The orc was choking him to death and asked, "How much do I get if I kill him?"

2

Ever since the kick in the head, the only thing that Iron Bones had known was fighting. He trained with his brothers day and night, with weapons of all sorts. He'd learned how to wrestle too. But he was far from a master of any of it, and it showed. His only saving grace was his strength.

Iron Bones buried his chin in the orc's hairy forearm and wedged his fingers between the brute's muscle and meat. Choking, he started to rise. His eyes locked on his brothers. Scar showed a sneer of victory, and Shamrok's eyes were filled with astonishment. Drysis was wearing a disappointed frown. *I'm better than this.*

His legs shook, but he rose higher. The orc was still covering him like a sopping-wet blanket. When Iron Bones looked at Scar, anger built inside him. His ugly sibling rode him all the time, never leaving him alone. *I won't give him the satisfaction.*

As his vision faded and his body flexed and trembled, the recesses of his mind recalled a fighting maneuver. He turned his hips suddenly and flung the orc from his back like a dog shedding water.

The wide-eyed orc bounced off the ground then skidded to a halt and struggled to rise. His chest heaved as he fought to stand. Putting a hand on one knee, he pushed upward.

Without hesitation, Iron Bones plowed into the exhausted orc. He grabbed the orc's arm and flipped him, sending him to the ground. Then he dropped an elbow on him. His fighting spirit caught fire, and he became another person. The orc was his victim. Bones broke, and limbs were twisted in their sockets.

The toughened orc wailed. "Mercy!"

But Iron Bones went to work. His ham-sized fist broke the orc's square jaw, busting his teeth. The orc crumpled on the dusty ground and balled up in the fetal position.

"That's it, Iron Bones! That's how you do it!" Shamrok roared. He pointed at the big-eyed human. "You! Earn your gold! Get in there!"

The man in leather armor had a wooden club with grooves and notches all over it. He leapt over the wall and charged Iron Bones from the flank, moving fast.

Iron Bones stood just in time to catch the full force of a mace to his skull. His knees didn't buckle the slightest.

The warrior paled. He held his club with both hands and struck again.

Grabbing the man by the wrists in a viselike grip, Iron Bones wrenched the club from his hands. It rattled on the hard-packed dirt. He head-butted the man, who stood there blinking, dumbfounded. Iron Bones head-butted the man again.

The warrior's knees buckled, and he swayed on noodle legs. All of the rigidness fled his body, and he fell sideways to the ground, holding his broken nose.

"Get in there, Lizard Face!" Shamrok yelled at the lizard man.

The lizard man was the tallest of the trio, with his scaly body rich in serpentine muscles. He slid over the wall like a snake and came in low.

Wary, Iron Bones crouched, holding his thick arms out at his sides with his fingers shaped like claws. His heart pounded like thunder.

The lizard man jumped like a jackrabbit and kicked Iron Bones in the chest, knocking him over. He locked his arms around Iron Bones's arm and pinned him to the ground.

Pain exploded in Iron Bones's shoulder, and it felt as if the lizard man was tearing his arm from the socket. He wanted to yell, but he held his tongue to the roof of his mouth.

Scar slunk away from the wall and squatted shoulder to shoulder with Shamrok. "Quit, boy! Quit! You can't fight, so quit!"

The lizard man twisted Iron Bones's arm. Stabbing fire-like pain burned through his shoulder. *No!* Immobilized, he hung on, refusing to yield. *No!*

"Iron Bones! Use your head, not your muscle!" Shamrok ordered. "You fight like a fool!"

"Heh-heh. He *is* a fool," Scar said.

They were right. He'd been taught better. He *knew* better. *Execute, fool!*

Iron Bones flexed his arm and shifted his hips. The lizard man hissed and cranked up the pressure. Pain bit deeper into Iron Bones's shoulder. His entire arm was burning. Gritting his teeth, he rolled to his feet, using the lizard man's armlock to brace him. With excruciating pain coursing through his limbs, he came toe to toe with the lizard man. He twisted his hand free of the lizard man's grip and shoved him away. "Let's try it again," he growled.

The lizard man's tongue flicked out of his mouth, his slanted eyes narrowed, and he bared his teeth then lunged at Iron Bones's legs. Iron Bones leaned on the lizard man and wrapped his arms around the scaly man's waist. He picked the lizard man up and slammed him back to the ground. Air whooshed out of the lizard man's mouth. He seized the stunned lizard man and knelt, putting him in a headlock.

Shamrok shouted in his ear, "You've got him! Finish it, Iron Bones! Finish it!"

Writhing and straining, the lizard man arched his back and twisted. His sharp fingernails dug through the flesh of Iron Bones's arms.

Drysis strolled over into full view. Her stone-cold expression could freeze a man's bones. Iron Bones felt a chill run through him the moment she said, "Kill him. Prove yourself to your mother."

He cranked up the pressure. The lizard man's tongue stuck out of his mouth, and he let out a raspy wet sound. The hard muscles in his neck gave way. *Crack.* The lizard man died, and his body slid from Iron Bones's powerful arms.

The battleground fell silent, and the wind cooled his face. Then the silence passed and was replaced with clapping. Iron Bones and the Doom Riders turned around and came face-to-face with Riskers.

3

The Riskers, three in all, were wearing full suits of blackened plate-mail armor trimmed in hammered gold. Spiked knuckles decorated their metal gauntlets, and their smooth faces were drawn tight.

Drysis quickly moved toward them and bowed. "Commander Shaw, it is an honor. What brings you to the Doom Riders' haven?"

Commander Shaw was a middle-aged man, clean-shaven, with traces of silver in his wavy brown hair. His face was lean and angular, and his eyes were as hard as diamonds. He was accompanied by two Riskers, a young man and a young woman, who could pass for twins. Commander Shaw looked down his nose at Drysis and said, "You remember Dirklen and Magnolia."

"Yes, of course. We were introduced at the banquet,"

Drysis said. Her fingernails dug into her palms. No one ever visited the Doom Riders' camp, least of all the Riskers. She slid her gaze over the twins. "Welcome."

Dirklen sneered. His golden hair was wavy and his skin, pale. His sister, Magnolia, was much the same, with longer hair and the inquisitive look of a cat in her eyes. Neither one of them acknowledged Drysis with so much as a glance. Their attention was fixed on Iron Bones.

"That's him." Dirklen spoke with a venomous tone as he eyed him.

Magnolia crossed her arms and stood on her toes for a second. "It is him all right. No mistaking that oversize head. That's Fest—"

"Commander Shaw, a word in private," Drysis said quickly. "All of us."

Shaw raised an eyebrow. "Make it quick."

Drysis nodded at the Brothers of Destruction. All four of them, including Iron Bones, headed into the barracks.

She lifted her eyes to the imposing commander and said, "Yes, that is Festive... or *was* Festive. He called himself Dyphestive while he was on the run, but he is one of the Doom Riders now and goes by the name Iron Bones."

Dirklen huffed a snobby laugh. "Stupid name for a stupid boy. I told you that I saw him, Shaw. I told you he was alive." He spoke as if he were in charge. "He'll be coming back with us now."

"I beg your pardon?" Drysis said with her own authority. "He won't be going anywhere."

"How dare you speak to me like that?" Dirklen fired back. "I've slaughtered people for less."

"Dirklen, this woman would cut you to ribbons. Stifle your tongue now," Shaw ordered.

"It is you that should mind yours," Dirklen fired back, "old man."

Commander Shaw backhanded Dirklen across the face. The stunning blow knocked the youth backward. Dirklen's cheeks turned as red as an apple, and he drew his longsword. Shaw shot a bolt of energy out of his hand and struck the sword. Blue tendrils of energy spread all over it.

Dirklen held onto the sword as long as he could, but then he screamed and dropped it. He fell on his knees, his gauntlets smoking. "I'll kill you for that!"

"Brother, quit making a fool of yourself," Magnolia said. "We came to talk, not fight." She poked Shaw in the chest. "But you shouldn't do that."

"No, I should have done worse." Shaw fixed his attention on Drysis while Magnolia helped her brother to his feet, but he stood and pushed her away. "Explain how Iron Bones came to be under your command. He is an escapee. He should be killed."

"Yes, killed!" Dirklen said as he picked up his sword and shoved it into its sheath. "Killed now. Immediately!"

If Dirklen weren't a Risker, Drysis would punch him in

the jaw. He was more obnoxious than Scar had ever thought about being. "Iron Bones was put into my care under Black Frost's orders." She looked down at Dirklen. "If you have an issue with it, you can address it with him."

"Oh, don't think for a moment that we won't," Dirklen said.

"Where is Dindae?" Magnolia asked.

"Pardon?" Drysis replied.

"Festive was joined at the hip with Dindae, an elf, who escaped with him. Where is he?"

"Dead," Drysis replied.

A frown formed on Magnolia's face, but it went away quickly.

"The Doom Riders were charged with bringing the pair back dead or alive. The elf didn't make it."

"Good," Dirklen said as he crossed his arms. "I hated him too. It's a shame that you and your rejects failed to dispose of the other, but I'll see to that if I have to."

"Drysis, you will need to accompany me to see Black Frost. It's imperative that we have this matter properly resolved," Commander Shaw said. "After all, Festive... or Iron Bones, rather... was being groomed to be a Risker. Not a Doom Rider."

"I'm well aware of that, but he has passed beyond the age of ripening. I don't think that he would do the Riskers any good now," she said.

"Yes, kind of like you and your rejects." Dirklen

strolled over to the orc, the human, and the lizard man, who were still lying on the ground. Though he was young, he was as well-built as a full-grown man. "Look at that. He only killed one of them. I'd have easily killed all three."

"Be my guest and finish the last two if you wish," she offered.

He turned toward her and said, "Perhaps I'll finish *you* off."

Seething, Drysis stayed silent.

"Dirklen, bridle your tongue," Shaw commanded. "Drysis, come with us."

DRYSIS and the Riskers were long gone, leaving Iron Bones alone with his brothers. They moved outside, where the battered and broken orc and human loaded the dead lizard man into the wagon and rode away empty-handed.

As Iron Bones watched them go, he felt empty inside. His victory was hollow. Something wasn't right. Not only that, but he wanted to know more about the Riskers who'd stared at him with burning eyes. It was like they knew him, but he didn't know them.

Shamrok put his heavy hands on Iron Bones's shoulders. "You did well, very well. Ha-ha, I'm twenty chips richer to show for it."

"He still fights like a swamp walker," Scar said. "If he wasn't as strong as an ape, he'd be dead."

"We all have our gifts. His is strength." Shamrok patted Iron Bones's back one more time. "Don't listen to him. Those men you fought weren't a bunch of street urchins. They were former soldiers, Terror Troops, that fight for a living. As tough as any under the rock. Except us, of course."

"And the Riskers," Scar added as he pulled a dagger from a sheath wrapped around his shoulder. He tossed it in the air and caught it. "I've never seen anyone talk to Drysis like that before and live. I was waiting for her to kill the boy."

Shamrok agreed. "If it weren't for their dragons, they wouldn't be so boastful. Nothing worse than a cocky youth. Ah, I remember those days. Anyway, so far as I'm concerned, Iron Bones is ready. He might still be rough around the edges, but I know that I can count on him in a fight."

His red-haired brother's words made Iron Bones feel good. "Of course you can. And I know I'm ready. Ready for anything. Even dragons."

"That's the kind of talk I like to hear." Shamrok took out his coin purse and started jingling them. "Ah, nice and heavy, how I like it. I can taste the finest ales and smell the pretty ladies already. When she gets back, it will be time to go. I feel it."

"What will we do?" Dyphestive asked.

"The same thing we always do. Hunt down Black Frost's enemies. Capture or kill traitors. And perhaps we find some treasure along the way that will set us up like kings," Shamrok said with a glint in his eyes.

Iron Bones nodded, though in his gut, he felt uncertain.

"You always were a dreamer, Shamrok." Scar flicked his dagger into the ground. "We'll have no more later than we have now."

"Drysis says that once the conquest is over, we'll all have lands of our own," Shamrok replied.

Scar picked up his dagger and said, "The only land we're going to inherit is a hole eight feet long and six feet deep." He pointed his dagger at Iron Bones. "Listen to me. Once we ride, you'd better not fail us, or I'll personally put an end to you."

Iron Bones wasn't sure why a brother would say that. He glared at him and said, "I won't fail you or anyone. I am Iron Bones."

4

Commander Shaw escorted Drysis toward the top of Black Frost's temple. He'd left the twins, Dirklen and Magnolia, behind. The climb up the frost-slick stairs that switched back and forth up the ziggurat's spine was long, and the icy wind kissed their faces.

"I'm not accustomed to taking the stairs. Typically, I ride my dragon. To my shame, this trek winds me," Shaw said as he looked down. They were over one hundred feet high, and there was nothing but jagged snowcapped rocks below. "I could use the exercise. Riding a dragon can spoil you."

"I wouldn't know," she said, her frosty breath visible. The climb to the top was miserable, even for the most durable people. It didn't help that both of them were in full armor, either. "So, how did you know about Festive?" She'd already brought Shaw up to speed about the gourn kicking Iron Bones in the head at the stables.

"Dirklen spotted him from above, of all things. The youth is as sharp-eyed as he is sharp-tongued. If you'd used more discretion, we could have avoided all of this."

"After so many years, I figured that he would have changed."

Shaw stopped on a landing. "One thing is certain—*you* haven't changed." He put his hands on her shoulders. "You are as beautiful as ever, Drysis. The truth be told, I've been looking for a reason to search you out anyway. I've never stopped thinking about you. You are always with me."

"And you are always married," she said as she lifted his hands from her shoulders and moved on.

"I erred. I know that now," he said. He grabbed her wrist. "I see you, and fire runs through me."

"Fire runs through me as well. The fire of a spurned woman. You chose her over me." She turned and faced him. "I'll never forget it. Don't bring it up again, *Commander* Shaw, or I won't be able to control myself, and you'll be kissing the snow on those cliffs." She pointed below.

"You always did have a way with me that no other woman had."

"Give it up." She marched up the steps, taking the lead. Over a decade ago, she and Shaw had been intimately close. They'd trained together to become Riskers, but when the dragons spurned her, Shaw chose another woman over her, a Risker named Adalia.

Shaw sighed and followed her.

Hundreds of steps later, they reached the top of Black Frost's mountain temple. It was a humongous plateau that stretched over one hundred yards in all directions. Dozens of middling dragons were perched on every section of the wall, facing outward. Black Frost's gigantic body, which dwarfed the middling dragons, filled most of the square. They were little bigger than his paws, which rested beneath his girth.

Black Frost's scales were as dark as coal but shone blue in the daylight. Each and every scale was bigger than a knight's shield. The hard ridges on his back were like hill-sides. His horns were dozens of feet long. They curled over once and went straight back. His head was resting on the ground. A village of people could have stood on it. He slowly opened up his eyelids.

Drysis and Commander Shaw quickly kneeled and bowed.

"Welcome, Commanders," Black Frost said out of the side of his mouth, revealing his teeth, which were longer than Drysis or Shaw were tall. "We have business."

Commander Shaw spoke. "Your Grand Majesty, I have recently discovered that one of the striplings that escaped is now in the custody of Drysis and her Doom Riders. The penalty is death for the boy, but I have been informed that you superseded that law. I came for veri-fication."

"This is true," Black Frost said. His head turned toward Drysis. His blue eye, as bright as a shining gemstone, probed hers. "How is the son of Olgstern Stronghair?"

"He is now Iron Bones, a Doom Rider. He knows nothing else," she replied, seeing no sense in giving Black Frost details. He didn't mince words. He commanded. You did.

Black Frost lifted his neck up from the ground and twisted it from side to side. His nostrils flared, and warm steam came down on the commanders. His chest expanded, and the plates of his scales flexed in and out.

Drysis had been in the service of Black Frost since she was young. At first, he'd been little bigger than a grand dragon, of which there were many, but over the years, he'd grown bigger and bigger, becoming the monstrosity that he was today. How, she did not know, and she couldn't imag-ine, either. It was her will and pleasure to serve.

"The time has come to move my ambitions forward," Black Frost said. "The Doom Riders will hunt down and slay my enemies, whether they be members of the Wizard Watch or the fools that hunt the dragon charms. I want them all dead."

"As you wish, Grand Majesty," Commander Shaw said.

"Commander Shaw, I've been informed that Riskers were lost near Lake Flugen," Black Frost said.

"It is true, Grand Majesty. Our search continues for Blackstone and his men. I have no doubt that the Sky Riders are behind it. In the meantime, we continue to torment the people of the countryside and search for their secret location." Shaw punched his fist into his hand. "We will find it and annihilate them all. I swear it."

"Don't trouble yourself with the Sky Riders. I don't want to lose any more Riskers. Pull back from the country."

Commander Shaw blinked hard. "Grand Majesty, might I inquire why? I feel we are so close."

Black Frost's eyes narrowed. He lifted one of his great paws and scraped his talons together. "Perhaps I know where they are. I await my spies to confirm it. In the meantime, lie low. I don't want them to suspect the frost that is coming."

5

GUNDER ISLAND

H idemark

IN ONE OF Hidemark's many rooms, Grey Cloak was sitting on a bed, holding Anya's hand while Yuri dabbed a wet cloth on the comatose woman's brow. Since the dragon battle over Lake Flugen, he'd sat with her every day, though his training had resumed. He eyed the gnome Sky Rider Yuri Gnomeknower, who was standing on the bed, making her as tall as he was, and said, "Why won't she wake up? I thought that you healed her."

Yuri scrunched her wizened face and sighed. "Her wounds are closed, but the cut was a fatal one. She lost so much blood that she should have died. She is breathing on her own—that's all that matters. Keep talking with her. I'm certain that she hears you."

"I'm pretty sure she'd rather hear from anyone else but me. After all, I'm the one that almost got her killed."

"Don't be foolish. Anya chooses to do what she does." Yuri wrung the water out over a bowl on the nightstand then set the towel aside. "I don't think that she would like to listen to you blaming yourself. She doesn't care for whining. You know that."

He nodded. Things weren't the same without Anya around. Even though he'd adjusted to the others, he truly missed her. She was beautiful and strong and could be friendly when she wanted to be. He touched her cheek and said, "If you don't wake up, I'll become the worst Sky Rider ever. You don't want that, do you? It would be your fault, you know."

With a twinkle in her eye, Yuri looked at him and said, "That's better." The short woman hopped off the bed and strutted away. She raised a stubby finger and said, "Don't forget, we still have a lesson today."

"Of course." With his eyes on Anya, he said, "You wouldn't want me to miss that, would you."

Anya's soft lips released a sigh, and she stirred.

Grey Cloak's body tingled all over. "Anya?"

She resumed her catatonic state.

He tucked the soft linens under her body. "Cinder misses you. He asks about you every day. He said to give you a kiss, but I'm not doing that. But I bet you'd like me to." He twiddled his thumbs. "Justus has been training me in sword craft, as usual, and Fomander makes me shoot the bow and arrow and toss spears all day. I've discovered that I'm much better with ranged weapons than melee weapons, and I don't sweat as much, either. The less perspiration to get the job done, the better, I say."

Seeing Anya lying in the bed tugged at his heartstrings. Despite what the other Sky Riders told him, if he hadn't tried to escape, then she wouldn't have been in that situation. Still, no one treated him any differently. They went on with the training like business as usual.

"They keep saying, 'One man falls, another must rise.' I think they are implying that I need to fill your boots. No matter how much they want to convince me that I'm a Sky Rider, I don't feel it. Sure, I'm Zanna Paydark's son, but what does that even mean? How can I be like a mother that I never even knew?"

"You can only go by what others tell you."

Grey Cloak turned.

Hogrim and Hammerjaw were standing in the doorway in full dragon-plate-mail armor, their hair damp with sweat. One looked as ironhard as the other.

"How is she?" Hogrim asked.

"The same."

The orc and the big-bellied dwarf eased into the room and stood on the other side of the bed.

Hammerjaw lifted a bushy brow and said, "She looks fine to me." He poked her. "Wake up."

"Don't do that," Grey Cloak said.

"What is she going to do? Slap me?"

"No, but I will."

"I'd like to see you try," Hammerjaw replied.

"She needs an orcen healer. They can wake up the dead." Hogrim jammed the towel into the water bowl. "Let me try something." He wrung the towel out over Anya's face. "Wakey, wakey. It's raining."

Grey Cloak snatched the towel out of Hogrim's calloused grip. "Will you stop it?"

"Why are you whispering? You can't wake her by talking." Hammerjaw made a cone over his mouth with his hands and shouted, "Anya, wake up!"

Hogrim did the same thing. "Wake up, Anya!"

"Stop it! Will you both stop it?"

"Yuri said to try something new," Hogrim said.

"New, not stupid. Get out of here, both of you. If you want to visit Anya, do it when I'm not here." Grey Cloak flung the towel in Hogrim's face. "Get out of here! Go take a bath or something. You both smell like a giant's armpit."

The heavily bearded Hammerjaw pointed a finger Grey Cloak's way. "I warned you about the giant jests. No one pokes fun at the giants but me." He nodded at Hogrim. "Come on. Let the elf sulk on his own. We'll see you in the morning. Come early. We have new recruits coming in."

"What?"

Hammerjaw turned. "You heard me—more whipper-snappers like you. We can't fight Black Frost with this small of an army. What did you think? That we were going to do it all on our own?"

"Well, no."

"About your mother—we both knew her well, and you have many similar qualities, but the one thing she had that we always admired was that she never doubted herself."

"What is that supposed to mean?"

Hogrim stepped back into view. "Stop being so whiny."

The duo walked away.

Grey Cloak hung around the bed and sulked for another hour, considering all that they had said and dreading working with new recruits. He still missed his friends in Talon, especially Dyphestive. Patting Anya's hand, he said, "I'm going to go now. I'm not whiny, am I?"

Her full lips parted, and she said in a barely audible voice, "Oh yes, very whiny."

Grey Cloak jumped off the bed. "Anya!"

6

Inside Hidemark's main corridor, Anya walked with a cane with Grey Cloak by her side. She was wearing a set of cotton robes and had a shuffle to her step. It had been over a week since she'd woken up. "This is humiliating," she muttered.

"Don't be silly. You are getting stronger every day. It was two days before you could get out of bed," he said. "You'll be flying on Cinder in no time."

She tapped her cane on the stone floor. "Huh! I can't even put my armor on."

"You don't need armor to fly a dragon, do you?"

"No, of course not."

"I don't see the need for armor, anyway. All it does is slow me down, and I don't want to be slowed down by anything."

"Sky Rider armor might look cumbersome, but it's very light and durable. If I hadn't had my armor on during my battle with Blackstone, there is no doubt that I would have been dead."

"Well then, it served its purpose. I'm glad of it."

"Me too." She stopped in the corridor and turned toward him. "There is something that I haven't told anyone."

"I'm all ears."

"I don't know how I killed Blackstone. He was better than me, but he told me something that set my head on fire." Her eyes watered. "He told me that he killed my father and my mother. At that moment, I was determined to kill him. I wanted vengeance."

"You got it. So what's bothering you?"

"It was all so sudden. I felt like I was in a dream and that my mind was not my own. I can hardly remember it." She leaned on her cane. "But now, I feel empty. All these years, I wanted to destroy Black Frost, only to find out that it wasn't him that killed my parents. It was Blackstone."

"Black Frost ordered their deaths. He ordered all of their deaths. It is our job to avenge them," Grey Cloak said, but he didn't have the same burning passion in him that Anya did. He'd never known his parents. For some reason, it was very hard for him to get riled up about it. "Black Frost will get his due."

Anya started walking again. Her cane clicked on the

stone and made a hollow echo that carried down the corridor. "Embarrassing," she said.

CLANG. *Bang. Slice.* Grey Cloak and Anya were going at it with longswords out in the jungle.

Her dragon, Cinder, was watching nearby. "You're dropping your guard, Anya. Keep it up."

Anya was breathing heavily, her red locks damp with sweat. She stabbed at Grey Cloak's head, but he parried easily and grinned. "Don't get cocky. I'm not trying to kill you."

"Obviously," he said.

Her strength was quickly returning. When they'd begun practicing, she could barely lift her sword. Now, not only did she wear her armor, but the strength in her limbs had hardened like steel. She was determined.

He cut over her head, and she ducked and sliced at him across the chest, but he jumped backward. She let out a painful groan and dropped to one knee, grimacing and holding her side.

"Anya!" He stuck his sword in the ground and ran to her. "What's wrong?"

"Nothing." She held a dagger to his throat. "Not for me, at least."

Grey Cloak's eyebrows rose. "Well, aren't you clever? But you might want to look closer."

She dropped her eyes. Grey Cloak's dagger was scratching against the skin of her neck. "Hmmm... it looks like someone is finally learning."

"Learning from the best." He sheathed his dagger and offered his hand.

She took his hand and stood up and groaned.

"You really are hurting, aren't you?"

"No, I'm fine."

Cinder crept closer. "Anya, what is wrong?"

"I said I'm fine."

"Anya," Cinder said in a warning tone. "Don't trifle with me. I'll whip you with my tail."

Grey Cloak giggled. "That would be something to see, a dragon turning Anya over his knee."

"Stifle it." She jammed her dagger into her sheath and said, "Blackstone's wound still burns. I felt something rip when I overextended."

"You're pushing yourself too hard, Anya. No wound so grave fully heals. You need to take better care of yourself. Rest more," Cinder said.

"I'll rest when Black Frost is dead." She stretched her arms behind her back. "I'm fine. As for you, Grey Cloak, I'm impressed to see how well your weapon skill has come along. It's far from the best, like me, but keep practicing, and one day, maybe."

"Maybe I'll be as good as you."

"I was thinking half as good." Anya threw her arm over his shoulders. "Come on. Let's see how the other trainees are doing." She petted Cinder's nose. "See you soon."

Together, they walked down the path back to the courtyard in front of Hidemark's temple entrance.

Hammerjaw and Hogrim were leading the new recruits in push-ups. The recruits were all elves, five boys and five girls, striplings dressed in leather armor. They were holding themselves up in the push-up position, and their arms were starting to tremble.

"Hold it!" Hammerjaw yelled. His belly touched the ground. "Hogrim, count down from thirty."

"Thirty! Twenty-nine! Twenty-eight!" Hogrim was also holding himself up. His body remained as still as a rock. Only his jaw moved. "Twenty-seven!"

Meanwhile, the trainees started to shake hard. Only a few of the elves were able to keep their arms steady.

"I don't miss that," Grey Cloak said. "Not at all. They ran me through those drills ten times a day. Ugh, my arms burn from looking at it."

Anya squeezed his arms. "Not too shabby. You were a stick before. It's about time you built some meat on your bones."

"Nineteen! Eighteen! Sixteen!"

"Seventeen," Hammerjaw corrected.

"What?"

"You skipped seventeen."

Some of the elven trainees giggled.

"What's that?" Hogrim shouted. "Looks like we'll have to start all over again. Thirty!"

The trainees groaned.

"Come on. Let's go back inside. I have something to show you," Anya said.

Grey Cloak smirked. "Me? A surprise?"

"It will be in your case, seeing how you surprise so easily."

He returned a dull "Ha-ha" as they entered the shaded sanctuary of Hidemark. "I have to ask… if we are being trained to be Sky Riders, won't we need dragons at some point? Not that I'm in any kind of rush, but the new recruits might be."

"All in due time. Like you, the recruits need to be prepared before they take to the skies."

"Where do they get a dragon?"

"You'll learn about that soon enough." She led him down the corridor into a huge room where the armory was located. Racks of weapons lined the walls along with a variety of suits of armor. There were enough weapons to equip a small army.

In the center of the room, between the worktables, a suit of blackened plate-mail armor was mounted on a wooden dummy. It was fashioned the same as the rest of the Sky Riders' armor, with many flexible plates and armored ridges. A helmet with dragon wings sweeping backward over the ears was sitting on the table beside it.

"Do you like it?" she asked.

"Uh, not really? I'm rather comfortable in my cloak." He poked it. "Feels bulky."

"Try it on," she said.

He eyed the dragon armor up and down. It was a beautiful suit, perfectly crafted to fit his body, but he shook his head. "No, thanks."

Anya's eyebrows knitted, then she picked up the helmet and shoved it into his chest. "Put it on, or I'll put it on for you."

With a sigh, he reluctantly placed the open-faced full helmet on his head then buckled the strap underneath it. He tilted his head from side to side and stuck his finger in the small earhole. "Did you say something?"

"Stop being silly. I know you can hear me. How does it fit?"

He took the helmet off and set it on the table. "I'm sorry, but I'm not wearing that." Without another word, he walked off.

7

FARSTICK

Rhonna the dwarf was trapped up to her neck in a pit of sand in the dry plains, the sun beating down on her face. She wasn't alone, either. Close by in the same pit were Lythlenion, an orcen cleric; Tanlin, the human rogue; Tatiana, an elven sorceress; and her henchmen, Razor the human blade master and Grunt, a Minotaur warrior. They called themselves Talon and had successfully stolen a dragon charm from a lizard king's tomb. While they were making their way back to Crack Scowl, a wild band of nomads known as the Dust Devils had come upon them and captured them all. Only the ranger, Bowbreaker, had escaped, but that was only because he wasn't with them at the time.

"It's a dishonor to die like this," Razor said. He white skin was sunburned, and his lips were cracked. "I'm supposed to die with my blade in my hands. You saw the quick work I made of the lizard men in that tomb. I turned them into chum. Now, well, I'm going to be scorpion food."

"Stop complaining," Rhonna said. They'd been baking in the sun for two days, and she barely had enough spit left to talk. "Save your energy."

"For what?" Razor asked sarcastically.

Grunt grunted. Tanlin was lying with his head on the sand and his eyes closed. He hadn't said anything in a day.

"This is my fault. I could have cast a dust cloud spell to cover our passage, but I hesitated," Tatiana said.

"Don't start blaming yourself. Everyone had a hand in our failure," Rhonna said, "and I'm no exception. We got cocky."

After weeks of seeking the lizard king's tomb, everything had gone according to plan when they got there. Talon had been well prepared. Lythlenion turned away the undead lizard horde in the bowels of the labyrinth of caverns, and Tanlin discovered and disarmed traps. When a multitude of wild lizard men came at them, Bowbreaker, Razor, and Grunt battered them to bits. The company churned their way into the murky depths of the lizard king's tomb, where they battled against a ghostlike spirit. Tatiana's gem of power tore it to shreds. They seized the dragon charm and some treasure but then came upon the Dust Devils, who took it all.

"It's sad to think that I'll never see my family again,"

Lythlenion said as he licked the sand from his lips. "Or have one last hot meal, either."

"Don't say that," Rhonna replied.

"Do you think that they captured Bowbreaker, too?" Lythlenion asked.

"I don't know," she replied. Bowbreaker was supposed to be scouting ahead, but they hadn't seen him before they were attacked. She still hoped that he was out there, though. He was the only hope they had.

The wind blasted into their faces. The nomads were a wild bunch of raiders, mostly orcs and men, that raided, pillaged, and moved on. They were as thick as thieves and had a cruel way about them. They left their victims as sacrifices to the desert, and the creatures of the sand would feast on the adventurers.

A small scorpion the size of a finger crawled across the landscape and made its way over to Razor.

"Go away, go away, little crunchy thing." Razor blew sand at the scorpion, sending it scurrying toward Grunt.

The Minotaur rocked his thick neck and snorted at the scorpion. The sand buried the arachnid momentarily, but it crawled out and away.

"Victory! You see? Things are turning in our favor," Razor said. "Even the desert critters fear Razor the Human Blade."

"Your reputation precedes you," Rhonna said dryly.

"It does, doesn't it."

Lythlenion, who was buried closest to Rhonna, said, "I think he's getting delirious."

"I don't think so." She gritted her teeth. Not only were they about to lose their lives, but they'd lost the dragon charm as well. The nomads wouldn't hesitate to sell it off to Talon's enemies. The entire mission had been a failure, and if anyone was to blame for it, she was. "I should have been more careful."

"They surprised us. I don't think anyone saw it coming. Not even Bowbreaker. And you know how good a scout he is," Lythlenion said.

"We should have taken another trail back. Instead, I rushed it, and we went back the way we came in. They were waiting. I can feel it in my gut. They saw us go in and waited for us to come out weakened. What a fool."

A train of small sand scorpions came back into sight. Dozens of them marched in a straight line.

Tatiana gasped and asked, "Will their stings kill us, Lythlenion?"

"They are small, and the stings are very poisonous. It will burn and cause delirium and hasten an inevitable and painful death, I suspect," the cleric said. "Sorry."

"I will try to summon a spell while I still have strength left." Tatiana squeezed her eyes shut, and her wine-colored lips started moving.

The scorpions crept closer and split up. In twos and threes, they marched toward the members of Talon.

"Tatiana, whatever you are going to do, do it quickly, please." Razor started blowing toward the scorpions in quick huffs.

A shadow passed over Rhonna's face, and she cast her eyes upward. Vultures were circling.

Suddenly, the sand started to shift. A beam of flickering light ripped through the sand and spread its rays into the scorpions, whose shells shriveled and burned to a crisp.

"Aha! You did it, Tatiana! You did it!" Razor exclaimed. "I'd kiss you if I could reach you! Zap go the scorpions! Ha-ha!"

Tatiana let out a sigh and managed a feeble smile. Sweat was beading on her lovely face, which was shining in the sun.

Then something blotted out the sunlight, and a shadow fell over all of their faces. Another scorpion crawled into their midst. Its tail was curled over its back, and the sharp tip dripped venom. It was flat, black, and huge—bigger than an ox.

"Tatiana," the wide-eyed Razor said, "I hope you have another one of those spells, because I think someone's mama's angry."

The giant scorpion's tremendous pincers clicked open and closed. It turned its body from side to side as its ebony button eyes scanned the company.

"If I only had a sword, I'd split that scorpion's shell open," Razor said. "Go away, bug! Feast on something your own size!"

"You have something to say in every situation, don't you?" Rhonna commented.

"Yeah. Is there something wrong with that?" Razor replied.

"Yes." Even though she agreed with Razor, she wasn't going to admit it. A young dwarf would rather die fighting than stuck in a sandpit or starving to death. The only honor in dying now would be for the scorpion to attack her.

Perhaps she could bite it. "Come on, you eight-legged spawn of the sands. Attack me!"

The scorpion shuffled in her direction and lined its stinger up above her head. A drop of venom dripped from the tip and sizzled in the sand in front of her face.

Rhonna crinkled her nose. The awful smell burned the hair in her nostrils. She hated to imagine what it would feel like if it stung her. Eyeing the monster, she said, "You missed."

"Be silent, Rhonna! Quit provoking it," Tatiana said.

The scorpion lifted its stinger higher then flexed, stiffened, and struck—just as a body of fur and feline muscle slammed into the side of it. A giant bobcat-like creature with a light coat of fur and dark spots clamped its jaws on the back of the stinger and tore it off.

The huge cat and the scorpion rolled over the dusty ground. Claws ripped at the scorpion, and the scorpion's pincers nipped off the cat's tail. The cat let out a painful mew and raked its sharp claws over the scorpion's eyes. Fur and black shell thrashed over the gritty earth.

Strong hands dug into the sand behind Rhonna.

"Get away from me!"

"As you wish," Bowbreaker said.

She caught a glimpse of his face. "Oh, it's you. Where in the forge have you been?"

"Escaping," he said as he hooked his hands underneath her armpits, then he dug his feet into the dirt and, with a heave, pulled her out. "We need to hurry." He glanced at the scorpion. "There will be others."

"Me next, me next," Razor said.

Rhonna helped Lythlenion out, and Bowbreaker pulled Tatiana free of the sand. All the while, the cat and the scorpion battled.

"What sort of cat is that?" Rhonna asked.

"A sand cat. Rare, but they thrive in these parts. I was fortunate to summon one. It pulled me out of a pit like yours after the Dust Devils captured me," Bowbreaker said as he lifted Tanlin out of his sandy grave. The older rogue's body was limp. "He's in bad shape but breathing."

"Some people can't take the heat. Now get me out of this sand hole," Razor demanded.

With the help of Bowbreaker, Lythlenion and Rhonna groaned as they pulled the hulking Grunt free.

The Minotaur stood upright and shook the sand from his body. He eyed the scorpion, which had broken free of the sand cat and was charging at it, and the cat's hackles were raised. Grunt jumped high and landed on the scorpion's broad back, squishing it. He stomped the monster into the ground with his hooves, and the scorpion's shell burst open, its guts oozing out.

The big cat sat on its haunches, licking its paws. Grunt ripped one of the scorpion's pincers off then grabbed the smaller part of the claw and ripped it open. He flung it away with a grunt.

Everyone else stood near Razor, witnessing the brutal scene, as Grunt stomped on the body again.

"What's everyone gawking at?" Razor asked. "Grunt hates bugs a lot. Now will you please pull me out of here?"

WITHOUT THEIR HORSES and with all of their possessions stolen, Talon moved on with little more than the clothing and armor on their backs. Following Bowbreaker, the party trekked over the dry land of Ugrad, chasing the nomad marauders known as the Dust Devils. They found the Dust Devils' camp three days later. The wild bunch of sand dwellers' tents were pitched in the hard terrain and sand. Talon was huddled in the rocky hills less than a league away on an overlook that gave them a full view. Night was falling.

"I COUNTED TWO SCORE OF THEM," Bowbreaker said. The sand cat was lying beside him. The elf ranger had nothing but his buckskins on. He might as well have been naked without his bow and his quiver full of black arrows. "There wouldn't be any shame in abandoning our possessions. We can go back to Crack Scowl and start over again."

"We have to do something tonight, or we will freeze our feet off out here. And we can't make a fire. Too much of a chance that their scouts will see it," Rhonna said as she eyeballed the camp. A corral had been set up for the horses, and theirs were among them. The tents were small, except for one in the center that was bigger than the rest. She hadn't seen anyone going in or coming out of it. "Share your thoughts, Tatiana."

"Every dragon charm matters." Tatiana wrapped her arms tight around her body and shivered. The north was a strange land, with searing heat in the day and air as cold as an ice troll's feet at night. "I've gained more magic the past few days. I can offer a distraction. We need to get that charm, Rhonna. That's what the Wizard Watch sent me for."

"We aren't all without assistance." Tanlin's jaw was sagging, but he was alert. His slender fingers rubbed the scarf on his neck. "In their haste and ignorance, the nomads missed the Scarf of Shadows. Perhaps I can slip into the camp and out with the charm. They might not even miss it until it's too late."

"Sounds like a plan," Rhonna said as she thumbed sand from the corner of her eye. "But we're going to need a backup to that one."

9

Razor paced, rubbing his hands together and blowing into them. "Once I get a sword in hand, I can take ten of those nomads myself. I think a bold attack would be better than waiting out here to ice over."

"Shh," Rhonna said. "Can't you see that we have work going on?"

Tatiana had created a fogbank that had begun to roll over the Dust Devils' camp, and using his invisibility and the cover of the fog, Tanlin ventured alone into the camp. The elven sorceress was on her knees with only the whites of her eyes showing.

Razor passed his hand in front of Tatiana's face. "As beautiful as she is, her ways are creepy."

Rhonna grabbed Razor by the wrist and yanked him

away from Tatiana. "Quit acting like a fool. Do you want to ruin her concentration?"

"No, I want to fight. I say let Grunt and me go in. We'll kill half of them before they know what's coming. Waiting for a thief to steal the dragon charm, and only the dragon charm, is a waste of time. I want my blades back and my treasure too. Those nomads have it coming."

"There are things more important than treasure," Lythlenion said calmly. "Settle yourself."

"Listen, orc, I'm a fighter. That's what I do. I can't help but feel naked without my weapons. What are we going to do if Tanlin does get the charm? Huh? Those nomads aren't fools. They'll ride us down." He punched his fist into his hand. "We need to strike when they least expect it."

"We'll get the dragon charm first," Rhonna said, squinting. She couldn't see a thing through the fog—not the tents, the horses, the nomads, or anything. "Then we'll see how it goes."

"Your plan will get us all killed," Razor said.

Bowbreaker put a heavy hand on Razor's shoulder. "Be silent."

"Or what?"

"Or else," the sullen-eyed Bowbreaker said.

Razor jerked away. "You're lucky I don't have my blades, or you'd be dead."

"You're lucky that I don't kill you with my bare hands."

Razor swallowed and walked off.

"How long are we going to give Tanlin?" Lythlenion asked.

"He said he'd be back within an hour," Rhonna replied.

"And if he isn't?"

Under her breath, she said, "I'll decide then."

In the background, Razor scoffed.

TANLIN CREPT between two nomad sentries. The wooly-haired men had their faces covered in scarves and their heads turned away from the biting wind. He turned and almost walked right into another nomad, but he slid to the side and passed. *That was close.*

With the fog that Tatiana had created coming in as thick as soup, a murmur started to rise in the camp. The nomads began lighting more torches. *Dirty my linens, I told them I didn't need the extra cover.* New orders were barked, and the guards were doubled around the perimeter. The Dust Devils were not fools. They were people of the wild and knew when something had a wizard's stink on it. But Rhonna and Tatiana had insisted.

Maybe I'm overreacting. For over twenty years, Tanlin had been practicing his skill as a rogue and had never been caught. But he was getting older, and his confidence wasn't what it used to be. He rubbed the edges of his scarf. *Thank goodness I have this.*

With soft steps, he moved deeper into the camp quickly. The course he set had him weaving through the tents until he came upon the largest one of all. He knelt at the back of the canvas and put his ear to the tent. A man with a raspy voice was whispering, and a woman let out a delighted squeal.

Tanlin's eyes brightened. It seemed that the commander of the Dust Devils was keeping company that night. He rubbed his hands together. The distraction should make his job easier. He snuck to the front of the tent. Two guards were talking about the sudden change in weather.

"I'll tell him," the larger orc said. They were both wearing desert robes over leather armor and had curved swords hanging from their hips. He shoved the smaller guard backward. "I'll bear the news. You go on. Do your duty." He pulled back the tent flap. "Dust King! A strange fog comes."

There was no reply.

The orc caught his breath and slowly stuck his head inside. "Dust King, I must tell you a—"

A fist smacked into his face. The orc stumbled backward and fell into the sand. A bearish orc, full of beard and heavy in shoulder and muscle, stepped outside, tying the belt on his colorful robes. A huge gold chain with a key on the end of it hung around his neck. He stuck his chin out and growled.

Tanlin shrank into a crouch and covered his head. The orc was huge and looking right down on him. He dared not look back up.

In a gruff voice, the orc said, "Mayla, get out!"

A petite woman who had long, silky hair and was wrapped up in a fox-fur blanket slipped out into the night and vanished in the fog.

When the larger orc guard stood up and saluted, the Dust King glared at him with his beady eyes and said, "Fetch my weapon."

The smaller orc dashed into the tent and returned quickly, carrying an unsheathed sword by the handle with two hands. The weapon was as long as a bastard sword with notched teeth on the back.

The Dust King took it and shoved the orc. "Come with me."

The pair vanished into the fog.

Tanlin's heart pounded like a hammer. He was used to slipping around, but the Dust King frightened him. They hadn't seen the massive orc when they were captured before. The brute, however, had an edge about him. He was a killer.

Better make this trip quick. He crawled on his knees into the large tent. A single lantern illuminated the canvas. On the ground were bedding, a large chest, metal plates, and mostly eaten scraps of food. The place smelled, too, reeking of sweat and body odor.

Tanlin gagged. *Ack. Apparently the Dust King doesn't wash very often.*

He remained motionless, with his eyes scanning the tent. It seemed odd that the Dust King would abandon his tent without leaving a guard, inside or out. There was nothing in the room that made him suspicious, only a hump of furs and blankets made into a bed. *The smell alone would keep his enemies out.*

Pinching his nose, he duckwalked to the chest. It was a heavy piece of furniture made of solid oak and steel fittings that time in the desert weather had corroded. He ran his fingers over the lock and rubbed his chin. "Hmm..."

Tanlin slipped off his belt and removed the lockpick set that was concealed inside a pocket in the leather. Using the two picks in tandem, he went to work on the lock. A few seconds later, it popped. *Perfect.* Then voices outside caught his ear, and he froze.

The big orc guard came storming inside and grabbed a metal breastplate lying on the ground, then he vanished back through the flap.

"This stinks of wizardry," the Dust King said on the other side of the tent. "Someone is out there. Probably the dervish enchanters sent to torment me. The Dust Devils will show them!"

Tanlin opened the chest lid slowly while keeping his face out of harm's way and his breath held. No darts or poison gas came out. He leaned over the chest. A familiar hoard of treasure was inside, including the dragon charm and more. He took the egg-shaped dragon charm in hand. The gemstone was warm to the touch, twinkled like fire, and sent a tingle through his arm.

I need to grab one more thing. His fingers stirred the loose coins and gems until he found Tatiana's Star of Light and pulled it free, the coins rattling.

As he started to close the lid, something in the room growled. He turned. A slavering desert hound, a large breed of mangy dog, had crept up behind him. *Oh my.*

10

Tanlin stopped breathing. His heartbeat felt like thunder in his ears. *Stop beating so loudly!*

Drool dripped from the massive dog's mouth. It was an ugly, shaggy beast covered in patches of mangy yellow-brown fur. Its shoulders and hindquarters were thick with muscles. Its muzzle was long, and it had a wet black nose with flaring nostrils.

Swallowing, Tanlin slowly dropped the lid back into place. The hound's head tilted to one side. Its drooping eyes drifted over the chest before landing back on Tanlin.

It sees me. How does it see me? In the back of his mind, Tanlin knew that wild animals had greater natural senses than men. The dog sniffed as it crept closer.

Of course... it can smell me. Smell my fear. A bloody dog, of all things! How did I miss it?

He told himself to calm down and breathe easy. His pounding heartbeat started to slow.

The hound's cold nose touched his neck, and its rancid breath was hot on his face. *Ew... that's awful. What do they feed this thing? Dead gnomes?*

Being mauled by a dog was no way to die. In fact, being eaten alive might have been one of the worst of Tanlin's fears. He had to do something quickly, while he was still invisible. If his or the hound's actions rustled him too much, the Scarf of Shadows would lose its magic.

The desert hound bared its teeth, and a louder growl rumbled in its throat. *I have to distract it. It's a stupid beast. I must be smarter than it is. And I have to warn the others.*

With the smelly dog in his face, he began to weigh all of his options quickly. First, he considered his bearings. The rocky hills that Talon was hiding in were south of the Dust King's tent. Once he got out, it would be a straight shot through the fog from there. Second, he had to fool the dog. He studied the lump of blankets that the dog had crawled out from under. It gave him an idea.

With every muscle on pins and needles, he slunk away from the dog. At a painstaking pace, he moved away from the dog and toward the heap of blankets.

The hound growled more and pawed at the air, then it began to sniff and dig at the ground. Head low, ears pinned back, it crept along Tanlin's path.

Tanlin grabbed a heavy fur blanket that smelled every

bit as foul as the hound. *How do they sleep in this stink?* He lifted the blanket and caught the hound's eye. The beast froze. It growled louder, reared back, and leapt.

He caught the beast in the folds of the blanket then bolted for the tent flap. Covering the beast gave him the moment of time that he needed. He ran as fast as his legs would take him. Through the fog he sprinted, the angry hound barking and nipping at his heels. He turned on the speed, but the hound closed in.

A clamor of voices rose in the camp. "Intruder!" someone screamed. "Intruder!"

Through the dense fog, he caught sight of nomads moving across his path. He aimed straight for them and said, "Hello there!"

They turned to face him, swords drawn. He dove between two startled nomads, and they caught the full force of the hound's jumping. The soldiers and the hound wrestled over the ground with angry shouting and ravenous barking.

Tanlin rolled back up to his feet. Though his invisibility was gone, his ruse had worked. The hound had attacked the soldiers. He took off into the night.

More shouts followed. "There he goes! There he goes! I see him!" The nomads had caught his trail and were in full pursuit.

From somewhere in the camp, the Dust King shouted, "Turn loose the hounds!"

This isn't going the way that I wanted it to go. At the rate he was going, he was leading the Dust Devils straight to Talon. He would betray them all. His only hope was to get the Star of Light to Tatiana. It was the only thing he could think of that would help if he could make it in time. *Run faster, Tanlin! Faster!*

The desert hound was still chasing him. It picked up speed and jumped. Kicking sand behind him, Tanlin took a hard angle to the left. The hound bit down on his ankle and pulled him into the ground. Tanlin screamed.

11

Rhonna popped up from her position behind the rocks. The Dust Devil camp had come to life. Wolfish hounds were barking in the darkness, and commands were being shouted. The wild nomads were coming. The barking became louder and louder.

"They've sniffed Tanlin out," she said. "Everyone hold your position. Razor! Grunt!" Her voice was a harsh whisper. The henchmen were scurrying down the rocky hill. "Stay put!"

Razor saluted. Grunt vanished into the foggy night, and the blade master disappeared with him.

Rhonna made a fist. "Those two have a death sentence." She shook her head. "Bowbreaker, go after them."

The rangy elf nodded then slipped down the hillside and was gone.

Rhonna was alone with Lythlenion and Tatiana. Her eye twitched as she looked at the elven sorceress and said, "You need to keep your henchmen under control. They're going to get us all wiped out. Even Dalsay and Adanadel weren't so brazen."

Tatiana said, "I'm sorry." Her delicate hands erupted with mystic fire. "If they survive, I'll be sure to have a stern talk with them."

"I'm sure that will go a long way." Rhonna would have rolled her eyes if it were her way, but it wasn't. All she could do was dig in and fight. "Lyth, I hope you have something worth more than a lick of salt."

The clamor of charging Dust Devils increased. Armor and weapons jangled. The brood was coming.

The orc had his hands pressed together in prayer, his eyes closed. "I'll do the best I can to protect us."

PAIN EXPLODED in Tanlin's ankle. He kicked the desert hound with his other boot, but the mangy beast shook him like a towel. He tossed his head back and groaned, waiting for his leg to be torn off. Fighting against the blinding agony, he kicked the dog in the face as hard as he could. *What a way to go!*

The hound started dragging him back toward the camp. Tanlin clawed at the ground. His fingers dug deep into the sand, but they found no purchase. He became numb, and his stomach turned sick. *I'm doomed.*

Grunt appeared in the fog with a snarl on his face. He reached down and grabbed the dog by the nape of the neck with both hands and squeezed. The hound let out a painful yelp, opening its mouth. Tanlin jerked his leg free. Grunt bashed the dog in the face with his horns, and the hound withered like a leaf and went limp in his hands.

Two Dust Devils pushed their way through the fog toward Grunt, brandishing their curved swords. Grunt flung the hound at the nearest nomad, knocking the man clear off his feet. But the move left the towering Minotaur exposed, and the second wild nomad swung at his chest. The sword came down in a swish, but Grunt blocked it, and it sliced into his bare arms.

Jumping out of the mist, Razor tackled Grunt's attacker, and they rolled over the ground. Razor ended up on top with his attacker's dagger in hand. He stabbed the nomad in the chest. Before the nomad's curved sword—a scimitar—slipped from his fingers, the blade master snatched it, and he stood with a blade gleaming in each hand. "Now it's my time to dance." He bolted into the fog.

"Get me back to camp quickly," Tanlin said.

Grunt's soft eyes looked in Razor's direction, searching the darkness.

"I have the stones, Grunt. Please take me now!"

The Minotaur lifted Tanlin into his muscle-bound arms

as easily as a man lifting a feather and dashed back to the camp. There, Tanlin found Rhonna, Lythlenion, and Tatiana waiting.

"I have the charm and the star," he said.

Lythlenion rushed over to him. "You won't have a foot if I don't tend to it. What happened?"

Grunt set Tanlin down on the ground.

"One of those desert hounds got me," Tanlin said.

Lythlenion fished a handful of nuts from one of his pouches and said, "Chew on these. It will numb the pain." He rubbed his hands together.

"What are you doing, Lyth?" Rhonna said. "What about our protection spell?"

"It will have to wait," the orc replied. "Those dogs are feral. Every moment counts, or Tanlin's blood will make him crazy."

"Great," Rhonna said. She picked up a rock from a pile she'd made. It was the only weapon she had. "Tatiana, the fog is fading."

"I know," the sorceress replied as she took the dragon charm and the Star of Light from Tanlin. The Star of Light glowed hot in her hand. The fog dissipated quicker, and their hiding spot was illuminated.

The sounds of battle at the base of the hill faded. The nomads were marching Razor up the rocky climb at sword point. They had taken the man prisoner.

Rhonna shook her head. "Horseshoes."

12

___

The Dust Devils scurried up the hill, and along with their dogs, they surrounded the camp. Rhonna stood on top of a boulder and eyed a wooly-haired orc making the trek up the hill with a bastard sword resting on his shoulder. He was wearing a suit of armor underneath his robes.

Tanlin peered down the hill and said to Rhonna, "They call him the Dust King."

Though Rhonna cleared her throat and started to speak, Tatiana cut her off and said, "Let me handle this, if you will." She stepped into full view, the gemstone glowing white in her hand. "That's far enough, Dust King!"

"Ah, you've heard of me," the nomad leader said in a gravelly voice. "But I don't take orders. I give them. Surrender, and I'll show mercy before I kill them."

Razor's arms were tied behind his back. The four nomads guarding him shoved him to his knees. One of them pulled out his sword and rested the blade on his shoulder.

"Take note that I killed five of them and one hound," Razor boasted. "One of them cowards got lucky and clobbered me from behind."

"Silence!" the Dust King said.

One of the guards whacked Razor in the side of the head with the pommel of his dagger.

Razor's face hit the sand. The nomads hauled him back up to his knees, and he shook his head as if to clear it.

"We have no quarrel with you, Dust King. We only wish for safe passage," Tatiana said.

The Dust King tossed his head back and roared with laughter. His brood joined in, and the hounds bayed like wolves. "You steal from me and kill my men, and now you ask for safe passage? The Dust Devils aren't known for their mercy. What we are known for is vengeance. All of you will die today."

Tatiana's gemstone burned brighter. The nomads shielded their eyes, but not the Dust King.

"I'm offering you a chance to live. Take it, or die," she said.

The Dust King let out a rusty laugh. "Huh-huh-huh." He looked around proudly at his men. "Does the little sorceress think that she can frighten me? The Dust King? I, who have killed dervish demons with my bare hands and eaten them for breakfast?" He held his sword out in front of him. "Go ahead. Try your trinket on the king of the sands and see what happens."

Rhonna and Tatiana exchanged nervous glances. The only hope that Rhonna could think of was Bowbreaker, but he'd vanished. Perhaps he and his sand cat were up to something. She hoped to see an arrow pierce the Dust King between the ears. *Where is that sneaky elf when you need him?*

Tatiana's eyebrows knitted. Her back straightened, and fierce determination filled her eyes. She glowered down at the Dust King and said with authority, "This is your last warning, Dust King. And I say that with the utmost respect."

"Huh. The Dust King is invincible. Try your best." He opened his arms wide and exposed his chest. "Try me."

Tatiana's fist charged like a ball of lightning. Fire shot down the hill and smote the Dust King full in the chest, but he stood as still as a mighty statue. The energy washed over his body like water with no effect. She clenched her fist, and her hand glowed hotter. More mystic fire poured out, and she opened her mouth wide and yelled.

The Dust King's body shook. He started marching up the hill with his sword cocked over his shoulder, going straight for her. Tatiana's eyes glazed over, burning with white luminescent fire.

He had a nasty victorious grin on his face as he closed the gap. "Prepare to die, witch!" He lifted his sword.

"Tatiana, move!" Rhonna ordered.

But the sorceress stood fast. With her jaw set and limbs shaking, she pushed more power out. The mystic force slammed into the orc.

With widening eyes, the Dust King screamed, "No, it's impossible!" He stepped backward as the white magic enveloped him. His robes deteriorated. The skin on his face shriveled and dried. The Star of Light's magic ate the Dust King down to the bone.

Then Tatiana's light went out, and the sweat-drenched woman collapsed on her knees. The Dust King was still standing, but nothing was left but his bones and armor. His mouth was opened wide, and the sockets of his smoking eyes were empty.

The Dust Devils retreated. Their hounds stopped their howling. Fear stricken, they fled.

Rhonna rushed over to Tatiana and wrapped her arms around her. "You did it. I don't know how you did, but you did—it?"

Tatiana's hands were shriveled and charred. She was crying.

13

DARK MOUNTAIN

Zora gave Deeann a big hug. "I'm going to miss you," she said.

The pie-faced halfling woman in a tall black hat hugged her back and said, "I'll miss you too. You were fine help, but I think the boys are going to miss you the most."

"Oh yes, I'd better say goodbye to them," she said as Crane pulled the wagon to the front of the tailor shop.

Zora's time in Dark Mountain hadn't been as horrible as she'd expected. She'd been well-fed and cared for. The people, generally speaking, were nice. But despite all of the accommodations, she could never fight the uneasy feeling that lingered in her. As close as she'd gotten to Deeann, she was ready to leave.

The halfling boys and men poured out of the front of

Deeann's tailor shop and piled on Zora like puppies, held her down, hugged, kissed, and tickled her.

Zora let out shrill laughs like a schoolgirl. "Will you stop it? You know I hate this!" Her belly tightened, and she burst out laughing again. "Stop it, puh-leeze!" she begged.

"That's enough, boys," Deeann said. She was dressed in her crimson overcoat with brass buttons. It gave the small, black-haired woman a commanding aspect. "It's her time to go, but she'll be back." She winked at Zora.

The ten halflings broke away from Zora and stood side by side in a line. All of them were wearing trousers and white linen shirts. They'd become little brothers to her, even though they were men. She hugged and kissed every one of them. "I'll miss you all." She wiped a tear from her eye.

With sad looks on their faces and their tiny hands in their pockets, the halfling bunch wandered back into the store.

Crane was dressed in his customary purple-and-gold-trimmed clothing. The paunchy man took a knee and shook hands with Deeann. "Thanks for taking care of her."

"It was my pleasure," Deeann said as she hugged him and patted his back. "See you soon, and bring her back anytime."

"I will," he said.

Zora and Crane climbed into the wagon, and the horse pulled them down the road.

Wiping a tear from her eye, Zora waved back at Deeann. "I really liked her."

"She really liked you too. Are you sure that you are ready to leave?"

She smiled brightly. "Mission completed. Dyphestive is alive and well. I only saw him twice, but he told me they will be out on a mission soon. All we have to do is wait."

Crane arched an eyebrow. "And how long ago was this?"

"A few weeks. I've been on pins and needles ever since, worried that the Doom Riders might slip out before I do. I've been keeping an eye on them."

"Well done. I guess it's off to Crack Scowl, then, to meet up with the others."

She eyeballed the wagon. It was barren, and it appeared that Crane was only traveling with the clothes on his back. "You aren't leaving with any goods at all."

"No. Dark Mountain's soldiers are a lot more thorough exiting than entering."

"I see."

"That's why I always leave with my wagon empty. I don't leave anything for the soldiers to search. I'd ride out of here naked if they'd let me."

Zora eyed him up and down. "That's probably not a good idea."

"Ouch, that's harsh. There are many women that enjoy a portly fellow. It's a sign of success and wealth."

"Or laziness and slothfulness."

Crane frowned at her and shook his head. "You've been hanging around Deeann too long." He cracked the horse lash. "Yah!"

14

GUNDER ISLAND

"For the life of me, I can't understand why you think it is so awful to become a Sky Rider," Anya said. She had her helmet tucked under her arm as she led the way through the forest. "It's infuriating."

Grey Cloak walked behind her, as quiet as a ghost. They'd been bickering ever since he'd rejected the Sky Rider armor. "Can we please drop this?"

"No," she said. "You are a natural and a legacy. You are meant to be a Sky Rider like the rest of us."

They made their way through the leafy forest, moving farther away from Hidemark. The trees were tall, with oversized colorful leaves. Spotted spider monkeys and black squirrels ran through the branches. Somewhere deep in the odd jungle forest, a lionlike creature roared.

He caught up with Anya and said, "Listen, it's easy for

you. You've always wanted to be a Sky Rider, but me?" He touched his chest. "I've always wanted to be... well, something else."

"A thief?"

"A wealthy elf."

"They say the wealthy make the best thieves."

"Perhaps they are hard workers," he offered.

"Perhaps." She frowned as she trekked over the rocks that lay in a wide creek. "You don't have your special gifts to make you rich. You have them to serve. They aren't for you."

He jumped from rock to rock, crossing the creek with ease, and passed her then began walking backward. "I might feel better about this once Dyphestive is with me. And I'm close to my anniversary."

"What anniversary?"

"You know, my rendezvous with Talon. It's almost one year, and I'm ready to go, if not sooner." He stopped and turned. Huge pink-and-white ferns covered the faded path. "Er, where are we going?"

"You'll see." She pushed past him and through the ferns. "I hoped that you would have given up on Talon by now. The truth is, Grey Cloak, you aren't like those people. You are different, and Sky Riders can't afford to have friends like them. We are our own family."

"Dyphestive is my family. Period. And I won't rest until I find him."

She rolled her eyes and said, "Of course not." Sighing, she made her way down a new path. "I suppose I would do the same for my brethren. After all, they are all that I've ever known. My true family."

"That's the first thing that you've said that's made sense in days."

"Watch it."

He smirked. "So, where are we going?"

"To the other side of the crater. Firestok has given birth."

"Really?" He ducked under some low-hanging palm leaves. "I didn't know she was pregnant. Come to think of it, I was so worried about you that I didn't realize I hadn't seen her in a while. So, does she have a lair nearby?"

Anya led him to a large pond that was being filled by a waterfall. Over one hundred fifty feet of clear water poured down from the cliffs and crashed into the rocks that stuck up from the pond. "This is Lethas Lagoon. Behind that wall of water is a lair. Firestok is waiting for you."

He tilted his head to one side. "Why?"

Several Sky Riders in full armor walked out from behind the falls. It was Justus, Aric, Stayzie, Mayzie and Yuri.

"What are they doing here?" he asked.

"Come on." Anya led him around the pond to the base of the rocks near the waterfall.

Everyone stared at him with serious looks on their faces.

Justus put his hands on Grey Cloak's shoulders and said in a somber voice, "The time has come for you to embrace your destiny. Inside the lair is Firestok. She has given birth to many. They are fledglings now, but they grow fast." He pushed Grey Cloak toward the gap between the rocks and the waterfall. "You are ready. Go now. Choose your dragon. Firestok awaits."

Ready? I'm not ready. Grey Cloak wanted to say that out loud, but he didn't. He didn't want to disappoint anyone, either. The Sky Riders' heavy gazes compelled him to move toward the lair. His time had come, and joking around wouldn't get him out of it. He took a breath and walked behind the thunderously roaring waterfall.

Two stone urns taller than men and with flames that burned green stood outside of the entrance to the lair. The backsplash and mist of the waterfall sizzled in the hungry fire. The stone ground was wet and slick.

Grey Cloak took one last look backward. He didn't see a soul. *No turning back now.* He wiped the cool mist from his face and went in.

ANYA STOOD shoulder to shoulder with her uncle, her heart

thumping. "I feel like I did the first time I went inside. I'll never forget it."

"No, neither will I," Justus said.

"I'm worried for him. He doesn't see right," she said.

"Agreed," Aric said. The mist on the slender elf's face looked like sweat, but his expression was as calm as always. "What are we going to do if he is not able to bond with a dragon? Do we kill him?"

Stayzie and Mayzie gasped.

"Brother, what is wrong with you?" Mayzie asked.

"I was only jesting, but... Justus, what do we do?"

Justus's eyes remained fixed on the splashing water.

Anya saw her uncle's jaw tighten, and she hooked his arm. "Uncle, surely we wouldn't kill him, would we? I mean, there have been others that have failed, right? What did we do with them?"

Justus blinked and finally said, "If he doesn't bond with a dragon, one thing is for certain—he can never leave this island."

15

Grey Cloak slunk into the lair with his shoulders slouched. The cavern was a gloomy abode with a ceiling that looked too low for a dragon to squeeze under. He searched the walls, looking for another avenue of escape, but the tunnel only went one way. His mind began to stir the farther he went. *They are forcing this on me, aren't they? I don't want a dragon. I don't like flying. And I don't want to be a Sky Rider. I want my life back!*

His thoughts didn't come without guilt. Grey Cloak knew that a war was going on and they needed help. He'd seen the carnage that the Riskers wrought when they destroyed an innocent village and its people. He even understood that he was part of a great legacy, but the truth was, he wanted to live his life too. On his terms and not someone else's. *We can't be the only people in the world fighting Black Frost. Let someone else do it.*

Smaller urns lit up the path that led deeper into the lair. He made it another hundred yards in when it suddenly opened up into a massive cavern complete with stalactites and stalagmites that reflected the urns' green flames. On the far side of the cavern, Firestok, a magnificent grand dragon, was lying on the floor. The scales on her body rose and fell. The more the plates expanded, the more the orange in her scales was shown.

"Come in, Grey Cloak. I've been waiting on you," she said in a motherly voice.

He crept forward and slowly weaved his way through the dampened stalagmites then stopped a few yards away, rubbed the back of his neck, cleared his throat, and said, "Uh... congratulations."

Firestok's burning-orange eyes brightened. "Why, thank you, Grey Cloak. Do you know that you are the only one to congratulate me? Well, the only person, that is. Cinder is quite happy."

"Oh, well, that's good." He'd seen fledgling dragons before. "They are very cute. Like you."

She batted her lashes. "Ah, Grey Cloak, you have a silver tongue, don't you?"

"I thought I did, but it isn't doing me much good these days. I like the Sky Riders, but sometimes I think statues offer better conversation. They only want to talk about one thing—Black Frost."

Firestok's tail swiped over the ground. Her fledglings jumped on for a ride.

She started to laugh. "They are very eager, this bunch." She dropped her huge head down in front of Grey Cloak. "What is wrong? I feel a sense of dread in you. Aren't you happy?"

"This is a great responsibility. I don't think I'm ready." He looked her in the eye. "Firestok, I don't want to be a Sky Rider."

"I see," she said with disappointment. "I like you, Grey Cloak, and I would trust you with my children, because I know that you would take care of them. I think you would be wise to not pass on this opportunity. It may never come again."

"What if none of the fledglings accepts me?"

"That is what we are here to find out, isn't it?"

She pulled her tail in Grey Cloak's direction and curled it around the fledglings, then she made a low growling, rattling sound in her throat. The fledglings nipped at one another with tiny razor-sharp teeth before they settled down inside the curl of her tail. They weren't very long, only a few feet from nose to tail, and their bodies weren't any bigger around than a hedgehog's. Their bright eyes locked on Grey Cloak as he approached.

He kneeled. "I never saw so many in the dragon kennels

at Dark Mountain. Each litter only had a few, but you have many."

"Perhaps that is because many are needed. Go ahead. Handle them."

Grey Cloak smirked. He'd partially raised the small dragons back in his time at Dark Mountain. Mostly, he and Dyphestive had fed them and picked up after them. "At Dark Mountain, the Riskers would tease us when they came. They called us the poop scoopers. I hated that."

Firestok gave a pleasant giggle. "I never heard that one before."

He inched closer, his gaze swiping over all of them. "Many of the dragons found riders after they were fully grown. Not all but many." He picked up a dragon. It squirmed in his hands and hissed at him, so he set it back down with the litter. "Can't I have a full-grown dragon like you?"

"It's best this way. But if you lose a dragon, that doesn't mean that you can't ride another. It's not the same bond, however," she said. "Many riders use the dragon charms to control them. That is only temporary, not permanent. Some riders, even with a charm, can't ride a dragon if it won't let them. Dragons are very... unpredictable."

Grey Cloak picked up one after the other. All of them hissed and wriggled out of his grasp. "I don't think this is going so well."

"You should talk to them that same way that you talk to me. Nicely."

"I'm an elf. I think they are too young to understand me."

Most of the dragons appeared the same. Their scales were slick and shiny, and their eyes were round and bright. Grey Cloak reached in and picked up the largest one. "He's heavy. And fat." He ran his eyes over the dragon's back. It had two black stripes running from the tip of its head down the back. It looked at him with dull eyes that weren't bright like the others'. Its pink tongue flicked out of its mouth.

"Say, it's not hissing at me or squirming," he said curiously.

"That's because he's the runt. He won't get much bigger than he is. I would leave that one alone if I were you. The others are a fine mix of middlings, and there are two grands among them."

"If he's the runt, then why is he the biggest?"

"He hatched last. For some reason, the runts are slow and big when they are fledglings, and they tend to stay that way. It is the natural order of things. I have a litter of eleven. One is the strongest, and one is the weakest. The others are evenly matched, mostly. And sometimes there is a runt and a grand, and sometimes there isn't either. Don't you want a dragon that will be grand like Cinder and me?"

Grey Cloak started to put the runt dragon back in the

litter. His tongue flicked out of his mouth again, and it made a funny *phlllyt* sound.

"So, I won't be able to fly on him?" he asked.

"Never."

"And he won't get much bigger?"

"I'm afraid not."

Grey Cloak gave the biggest smile he'd smiled in weeks and cradled the dragon against his chest. "Perfect. I'll take him!"

"You'll what?"

"I said I'll take him. No offense, Firestok, but as far as I'm concerned, this dragon is perfect for me."

Firestok's great jaw dropped. She ran her paw along her snout in disbelief. "In all of my years, I have never heard of anyone choosing a runt. They are turned loose into the wild."

"Well, you know what they say," he said in a chipper voice. "There's a first time for everything."

"He'll need a name," Firestok said with a sigh.

Grey Cloak held his dragon up high. "I'll call him Streak."

Firestok nodded. She kissed her runt dragon on the top of the head and said, "This is where I'd customarily say, 'Ride the Sky,' but it seems very inappropriate. Go with my blessing, Grey Cloak and Streak. And remember, you can always come to me."

Grey Cloak hurried away like a child that had just received a new toy. "I can't wait to show them."

Firestok laid her head down and cradled her fledglings' bodies to hers. "I'd do anything to capture pictures of their faces. It will be a scream."

16

"A runt? A *runt*?" Hammerjaw banged his fists on the table. "This is madness! What sort of Sky Rider takes a runt of a dragon? I say that Grey Cloak must go!"

All of the Sky Riders were silent. They were deep inside Hidemark's temple, behind closed doors, sitting around a circular marble table. Anya, Justus, Aric, Stayzie, Mayzie, Fomander, Hogrim, and Yuri were present. All of them wore frowns on their faces.

Anya stood and said, "Just because he chose a runt doesn't mean that he needs to be banished. Perhaps it is a good thing."

Hammerjaw flung his hand outward. "It is preposterous! Period! A runt dragon is good for nothing."

"That's not entirely true," Yuri Gnomeknower said.

"Some of them are very smart, and they make excellent pets."

Hammerjaw stood on his chair, put his knuckles on the table, and glowered at her. "A pet? Is that what we are fighting the war against Black Frost with? Our pets? As much as I would desire to embrace Grey Cloak, face it—he does not belong. He is nothing like his mother. He must go!"

"He can't go," Aric said as he stood up. "He knows too much."

"And what would you have us do? Keep him prisoner?" Anya asked.

The Sky Riders broke into several heated conversations, yelling and screaming and shaking their fists at one another. Grey Cloak's surprise had all of them at one another's throats. The only one that wasn't saying a word was Justus. He sat in his chair, pulling the hairs on his beard, listening. Back and forth the parties went. Aric's face was as red as an apple. Veins bulged in Hogrim's neck. Yuri talked nose to nose with Fomander. Everyone but Justus had something to say.

Anya defended Grey Cloak to the elven trio. "He has a dragon. He's one of us now!"

"It's a runt!" Aric said smugly. "You're being ridiculous."

"He can't leave the island," Stayzie said. "He has no choice but to stay. He can still help us."

Anya's temper boiled over, and she yelled, "We gave our word that he could leave!"

"That's changed!"

"No, it hasn't!"

"He needs to be imprisoned!"

Anya felt like her head was going to explode. She was the only one defending him. Flinging her hair out of her face, she turned to Justus. "Well, Uncle, what do you think?" she shouted.

The group fell silent. Justus—the leader of the Sky Riders—sat up in his chair and leaned forward with his elbows on the table. He scanned all of their faces and said calmly, "Has everyone flushed their opinions from their systems? Or do we want to continue squabbling like halfling merchants?"

One by one, everyone at the table pulled back their chairs and sat down.

"He can't be let loose, Justus," Hammerjaw said.

Justus lifted his hand. "Please, keep silent. I would like to share my thoughts." He took a breath and said, "As disappointing as this is, can any one of us find anything that Grey Cloak has done wrong? He went into the lair, and he came out with a dragon. That was what was expected of him."

"But Justus," Aric whined.

"No, let me finish. Grey Cloak was given a choice, a

choice that we forced him into. Now, I know that we all have great expectations for him, given that his mother was Zanna Paydark. However, he is not her. In order for us to get the best result, we should guide him." He closed his eyes for a moment. "I fear that we have failed to guide him. Either that, or his opportunity has passed since he missed the ripening. But he is still a natural and not without his use."

The Sky Riders exchanged looks.

Yuri spoke up. "What are you suggesting, Justus? That we let him go? He knows too much about us."

"Black Frost believes that he is dead. He won't be looking for him," Anya interjected.

"What are we supposed to do? Let him walk about Gapoli with a dragon?" Hammerjaw huffed. "That will raise suspicions."

"Plenty of people keep runts as pets all over the world. Certainly, it is rare, but it is far from shocking," Anya said. "Besides, I trust him." She glanced at her uncle. "I'm sure Firestok does too."

Justus nodded. "Perhaps." He stood with his knuckles on the table. "Every year, we take new counsel and elect a leader. I'm honored to fill that role. You have trusted me to have the final say in our direction. In some cases, for the sake of unity, I put our decisions to a vote. It seems that we are very divided on how to handle Grey Cloak. Even I am wrestling with the decision." He looked down at the table before looking back up. "In this case, I am going to put it to a vote."

"Uncle, no!" Anya said.

Justus lifted his hand. "Hear me out. I want every one of you to give careful thought to all that we have discussed. I won't stand here and stump one way or the other like a monarch politician. I respect all of you and your decisions. Search your hearts." He scanned all of their faces and paused. "All right then. By a show of hands, who is in favor of Grey Cloak and his dragon remaining on Gunder Island?"

Hammerjaw and Aric were the first to lift their hands. Stayzie raised her hand as well as Mayzie.

Anya's fingernails dug into her palms. There were nine Sky Riders, and five made a majority. They only needed one more vote, and Grey Cloak's fate would be sealed. Justus's hand started to move.

17

Grey Cloak waited outside in a forest grove as he was told. Cinder and his runt dragon, Streak, were with him, and Cinder was lying on the ground, watching Streak crawl along the ridges of his back.

"Aw, I wish you could have seen their faces, Cinder. When they realized that Streak was a runt, I could have sworn their heads were going to explode." He was lying in a bed of grass, laughing. "I swear Hammerjaw's beard almost fell off. If only I could draw a picture of it."

"Yes," Cinder said. His golden eyes were rolled up in his head so he could watch Streak try to nestle behind one of his great horns. "Don't you think you took your decision lightly? It seems that you made it more out of spite than for a useful purpose."

Grey Cloak rolled over to his side and faced the grand dragon. He put a long piece of grass in his mouth like a pipe. "I don't think I did anything wrong. First off, I picked up many of the fledglings. They squirmed like fish out of my hands. They even hissed at me." He reached out and let a large blue-winged butterfly land on his finger. "Nothing felt right from the moment I entered the lair. It really didn't."

Streak crawled down Cinder's nose. His eyes were slits as they locked on the butterfly, and his tongue flicked out of his mouth.

"The truth is, I was about to give up," Grey Cloak continued, "when Streak's stripes caught my eye. He was hunkered down in the curl of Firestok's tail, not squirming around like all of the others. And he looked fat, sort of flattened out like a toad. When I picked him up, I fully expected him to claw his way out of my grip. Instead, he didn't budge, like he was stuffed. The only thing that moved was his tongue. His eyes met mine, and I swear he was looking at me like I was... stupid."

Streak crept along the ground toward Grey Cloak. His pink tongue flashed out of his mouth and snatched the butterfly. He gobbled the insect up and licked his chops.

Grey Cloak reached over and picked up his dragon then lay on his back and held him up like a puppy. Streak's scales were still soft and slick like a snake's. His eyes were dull and black. The little claws on his paws were flexed, but he didn't move, and his tail was as stiff as a board.

"Anyway, I like him. I think he likes me. He sort of reminds me of Dyphestive, seeing how he's built like a block of wood and heavy like an anvil." He lowered the dragon to his chest, and Streak's claws dug in. "Ow. Easy, Streak. I don't have scales like you."

Streak's grip eased. He laid his head down and flattened out on Grey Cloak's chest.

Petting his dragon, Grey Cloak said, "I know that they are mad at me and that I should care more, but I don't. Is that bad?"

"No, it was your right to make the choice that you made," Cinder said with breath as warm as toast. "And I don't think that your choice turned out the way anyone expected. If anything, I believe that they thought you wouldn't return with a dragon at all. That would have been a much worse scenario than this."

"So, are runt dragons, well, you know, useless?"

"No, of course not. They can be wonderful companions. Just because they are smaller doesn't mean that they don't have the same abilities as dragons. They can fly and even breathe fire in some cases. That is rare, because their bodies aren't big enough. And as you just saw, they have strong senses and are excellent hunters. Wherever you settle, I guarantee there won't be a moth or insect of any kind living in your cottage if you don't want it to be."

"Sweet bread, I like the sound of that. Of course, it's not very likely I'll go anywhere. I bet you anything that they are going to keep me on this island. I'm no fool. I could see it in their eyes."

"Either that, or they might kill you."

Grey Cloak jumped up. "What?"

18

"Thunderbolts!" Grey Cloak winced. His sudden movement caused Streak to bury his claws in his chest. "I need to remember not to move too fast. He's like a frightened cat." He pulled the dragon off his chest. Streak's claws clung to his clothing, but he released them. "Do you think they would really kill me?"

"If they find you guilty of treason, yes," Cinder replied.

"Treason? Because I took a runt dragon?"

"Perhaps."

"That's insanity." He gave Cinder a worried look. "Isn't it?"

"The Sky Riders are at war with Black Frost. They take every decision very seriously. You can't expect them to invest all of this time in you and suddenly let you go."

Cinder snorted. "It would be best if you worked with them."

"I'm trying." He stood up and stretched his arms. "Don't you think I'm too young to be in this war?"

Cinder shrugged. "The trainees are much younger."

"I get it—that's a bad excuse. But they volunteered. I didn't. I really want to get back with my friends and find Dyphestive." With his arms behind his back, he paced.

"And what if you discover that your friend is dead?"

Grey Cloak's heart sank into his stomach. "Well, that would be my fault, and I'd have to live with it. But in the meantime, we made a promise to look out for each other, and I vow to stand by it. I know that he would." His voice quieted. "He is a better man than me."

Cinder's head lifted from the ground. "Don't underestimate yourself." He looked beyond Grey Cloak's shoulder. "We have company."

Grey Cloak turned. Anya was marching down the path with a pack of gear slung over her shoulder. She was alone, and she had a grave look on her face.

He bent over to pick up Streak and held him to his chest like some sort of shield. "I take it that you have bad news?"

Anya's cheeks were flushed, as if she'd just come from a long argument. Her hands were shaking. "They don't understand. None of them do."

"Understand what?" he asked.

She looked him dead in the eye and held his stare. "As much as it pains me to admit it, I believe you are right. If your heart is not in this, then you should not have to do this. And you should be able to choose whatever dragon you wish."

"We chose one another, I think," he said.

"Yes, I know how it goes." She sighed. "Oh, if you weren't so hardheaded, this would be so much easier. All you needed to do was train with us and become a Sky Rider. Instead, you choose, well, your friend over us. I admire you for that. The truth is that I haven't known any other friends but them. But now, they are blinded by their desire to defeat Black Frost. We all should be, but with you, it doesn't feel right."

"Anya, what is happening? Are they going to kill me?"

"Heavens no." She trembled.

"What happened, Anya?"

"Justus had us vote on whether you would remain or if you could go. Hammerjaw, Aric, Stayzie, and Mayzie were the first to lift a palm. For several moments, no one else did. I thought you would be released. But Yuri raised her hand, followed by Hogrim and Fomander. Eventually, Justus did as well."

His throat tightened. "What happens now? I can't leave, even to rendezvous with my friends?"

She nodded.

"They can't do this. It's unfair!" He stormed back and forth with his bull-necked dragon cradled on his chest. "What am I supposed to do? Train as a Sky Rider? I won't be able to fly on my dragon."

"No, they aren't going to allow you to do any of that anymore."

He stopped and asked, "What am I going to do then?"

"Until they decide otherwise, you're going to be kept as a prisoner," she said.

"A *prisoner*? I haven't done anything wrong."

"I've been sent to fetch you," she said as she took a step toward him.

He backed away. "You're taking me to jail?"

"No." She walked right by him and climbed up and into Cinder's saddle, then she strapped her helmet onto her head. She stared at Grey Cloak. "I'm taking you away. Get on. We don't have much time."

Grey Cloak's eyes widened. "Are you sure?"

"Get on before I change my mind!"

He joined her in the dragon's saddle.

"Ride the sky!" she said to Cinder. "Ride the sky!"

JUSTUS WAS SITTING in the meeting room with his feet propped up on the table. His head was leaned back, and his eyes were closed. He was alone. He felt bad for his niece Anya. Her heart was in the right place, perhaps better than the others. She was young and not completely blinded by the mission to destroy Black Frost. The truth was, he agreed with her and thought that Grey Cloak should have been left free. But it was a time for unity, not controversy.

His decision troubled him. *I should have made the decision on my own.* At least, that was what he was thinking. At first, he'd thought Grey Cloak was safe, but when Yuri lifted her hand, it was all over. The others caved, and he did too. For unity.

The Sky Riders would be tasked with keeping a close eye on Grey Cloak. He'd tried to leave once, and he would try again. They had no choice but to imprison him for the moment. It was the only thing to do, even though it didn't feel right. He let out a long sigh that echoed hollowly in the big chamber.

Aric and Hammerjaw stormed into the room with frowns on their faces.

Justus swung his feet off the table, twisted around in his chair to face them, then leaned over the chair's arms and asked, "What's wrong?"

"It's that blasted niece of yours!" Hammerjaw said. "She flew away on Cinder and took that misbegotten elf with her!"

"We are ready to fly," Aric said. "Give the command."

Justice stood quickly and said, "No, she'll be back. Let her go. When she returns, she'll suffer the consequences."

"That's preposterous!" Hammerjaw said. "The elf is getting away."

Justus looked down at Hammerjaw. "He was already gone. My order remains."

CRACK SCOWL

Zora locked Tatiana up in a tight hug. Tears streamed out of her eyes. "I'm so glad to see you again."

Talon had met up with Zora and Crane in a tavern, Rooty's Rest, in Crack Scowl. It was the same dreary tavern they'd met in before.

Tatiana's embrace was weak, and her eyes were tired and heavy. "It's good to see you, too," she said weakly.

"What's wrong?" Zora asked as she pulled Tatiana down into her chair and sat beside her. The other members of the party were spread out, eating and drinking. She noticed the bandages wrapped around Tatiana's hands. "What happened?"

"I burned my fingers fighting the Dust King," Tatiana said. She gave Zora a quick account of everything that had happened on their quest to retrieve the dragon charm. "He was protected by strong magic. I used the Star of Light against him, but it wasn't enough, so I tapped deeper into the forces of wizardry." Her eyes brightened. "Such raw power. I've never reached so deep before. It nearly killed me, but instead, it killed him. A good thing."

Zora held her gently by the forearms. "Will you recover?"

"I am recovering, thanks to Lythlenion. If it weren't for his healing prowess, well, I might have lost my hands and my arms. I wouldn't be a very good sorceress then." She tapped foreheads with Zora. "I'm glad you are here. It's not so easy to bond with Rhonna. It's good to have another woman around I can talk to."

"You know that I'm here for you. Why don't you get some rest. You look so tired."

"I wanted to be here to see you. It warms my heart, seeing my little sister."

Zora teared up again. "You think of me as a sister?"

"I always have."

She sniffed. "Thank you... sis." She wiped her eyes as her gaze swept over the room. Everyone was present except for one person. "Is Bowbreaker well?"

Tatiana managed a feeble smile. "I think he'd rather die before entering a civilized tavern," she said. "You're fond of him, aren't you?"

Zora grinned. "Maybe a little. Of course, I've hardly spoken with him."

"Well, enough about him. Tell me about Dark Mountain."

Her eyes lit up. "It's fantastic. Beautiful. Every need is provided for, and the people are wonderful, mostly."

Tatiana blinked. "Yes, I've heard that it is very... seductive."

"That's a good word for it. It cradled me right in."

"So, you found Dyphestive?"

"I'm not sure that I found him so much as stumbled upon him, but yes. He's alive!" She squeezed Tatiana's forearm.

Tatiana winced.

"Sorry." She let go. "I can't wait to tell Grey Cloak. He'll be elated. Has there been any word from him?"

Tatiana shook her head. "None."

RHONNA, Tanlin, Lythlenion, and Crane were sitting together at a keg-barrel table near the fireplace, eating off metal plates layered with greasy meat and vegetables.

"I know this food is awful," Lythlenion said as he sniffed the plate, "but after this last journey, it's practically delicious."

Tanlin sipped his wine. "I can't thank you enough for taking care of Zora, Crane." He lifted his goblet. "Thank you."

Crane twisted around and eyeballed Zora. "She's a very capable young woman." He turned back. "The truth is, I was worried too. Dark Mountain can change people, but she remained unaffected." He lifted his goblet. "To success."

All four of them clinked their goblets together. Purple wine sloshed over the rims and onto the table.

Crane gave a cheerful giggle. "Now that everyone is reunited, how do you hope to corral Dyphestive from the Doom Riders? That's certainly a task that I don't envy. But I'll help any way that I can."

Rhonna lit a cigar on a candle. "I'm thinking on it."

"If you can," Tanlin said, "I'd like you to journey to Loose Boot. That is where we told Grey Cloak to meet us."

"It's not a matter of if I can. It's a matter of if I'm willing," Crane said. His gaze slid over to Rhonna. "You wouldn't happen to have another one of those cigars, would you?"

She reached into her clothing and removed another cigar then handed it to Crane. "Enjoy yourself. They are made from dwarven leaf. Very stout."

"Interesting." Crane bit off the end and puffed the cigar over the candle flame. "How did you come by them so far north?"

"We found them in the Dust Devil camp along with their treasures and a few other items." She eyed Lythlenion's chest. He was wearing the breastplate that the Dust King had worn. The metal was solid black and had lightning bolt runes carved into it.

"If my eyes don't mistake me, those runes are the mark of the legendary blacksmith Thundell Misthammer. They say he was a master of wizardry too. You've come upon a true prize," Crane said.

"Lucky for me, I was the only one that it fit," Lythlenion said. He rubbed the breastplate. "I have to admit, I can feel the magic in it. This plate along with my mace, Thunderash, will make for a deadly combination. I'm ready to fight again already, and I consider myself a peaceful person."

Crane chuckled. "I can see that. As for Loose Boot, Tanlin, consider me already there. I'll be on my way at first light. Once I come upon him, I'll send him in your direction." He pushed a bright-emerald medallion over the table. "Hold on to this, and I'll know exactly where to find you." He stood and patted his belly. "Farewell, friends. I'm off to bed." He nodded, headed to Zora's table, kissed her cheek, and vanished up the tavern stairs.

Rhonna blew a smoke ring. "Now that Crane's gone, we have other matters to attend to."

Tanlin leaned forward with his hands clasped together on the table. "Such as?"

She eyed Razor and Grunt. They were sitting on the other side of the tavern, flirting with a group of barmaids. Razor had a charming smile on his face, and Grunt grunted with laughter. "It's time to part ways with them."

20

"You can't be serious, Rhonna," Tanlin said, aghast. "If it weren't for those two, I would have died. We *all* might have died."

"They disobeyed my orders," she stated matter-of-factly. "I'm not trying to be difficult, and I recognize what they did. They'll have their share of the treasure for it." She huffed out a stream of smoke. "But we have to be unified, and those two are dangerous."

Tanlin challenged her. "They're fighters. They are supposed to be dangerous."

"That's not what I mean."

"I know what you mean, but need I remind you that you don't make the final decision?" Tanlin took a long drink from his goblet. "Rhonna, you can't control every move we make. Fighters like that, well, they have a gut instinct. It's certainly not something that I have. I would think that you of all people would relate."

"I can relate fine. But orders are orders. Maybe they pulled it off this time, but what about the time after that and after that?" she asked. "We have to be a cohesive unit."

"We were desperate." Tanlin looked at Lythlenion. "Do you agree with her?"

Lythlenion finished chewing a mouthful of juicy beef, wiped his mouth on a cloth, and said, "I do."

Tanlin rolled his eyes. "Of course you do. You go along with anything she says."

Lythlenion poked Tanlin hard in the shoulder. "I hope you aren't implying that I don't think for myself. I wouldn't take kindly to that."

"No, I apologize. I should know better than to attack the man who healed me." Tanlin rubbed his eyebrow. "Razor and Grunt are Tatiana's henchmen. You know full well that she won't agree with you. Between the two, the decision will be split. Then what will you do?"

"We'll see." Rhonna pushed her chair back on its rear legs, whistled, and waved Tatiana and Zora over.

They took their places at the table.

Tatiana politely placed her elbows on the table and said, "What are we discussing?"

Tanlin opened up his mouth, and Rhonna cut him off with a hand to the face. "It's about your two henchmen."

"Yes?"

"I don't think they should come along anymore."

Tatiana tilted her head to the left and asked, "And why is that?"

"They don't follow orders," Rhonna replied.

"I see." Tatiana scooted closer to the table. "As I saw it, if they had followed orders, all of us would have been dead."

Rhonna's face darkened. "Is that what you think?"

"I don't think anyone else disagrees."

"I don't," Tanlin said.

Lythlenion spoke up. "None of us could have known the outcome if it had been otherwise. Not you or me or anyone. I don't think it's fair to say it could have gone one way or the other."

"Rhonna, I realize that Razor is bold and brash, but he is young and highly skilled. Grunt is not only a rarity but also a jewel to have as a companion."

"The point being..." Rhonna growled.

"We need them."

"Agreed," Tanlin added.

"This isn't a vote," Rhonna said. "I'm not going to put it all on the line with that pair acting on whimsy. I'll move along without them."

"Rhonna, please, be reasonable," Tanlin said. "If we cross the Doom Riders, we will need all of the muscle we can muster."

She looked Tanlin dead in in the eye and said, "That's my point precisely. We don't want to cross the Doom

Riders. But that pair, once they get a sniff of them, will rush in with their horns lowered. We can't have that. Getting Dyphestive back must be subtle. Sneaky."

"I'm not going to put them out in the cold," Tatiana said.

"They are men. They can handle it. Besides, they'll be leaving with filled pockets. Razor's even taken a shine to his new sword," Rhonna pointed out. "I'm not changing my mind."

"You're being unreasonable. Young men make mistakes," Tatiana said. "Stop being so stubborn."

"If you don't like it, you don't have to come along."

Tatiana stiffened. Her smooth forehead creased, and she took a deep breath. "Let me try this one more time. And I really hope that hard head of yours can make sense of it."

Rhonna blew a ring of smoke at her.

Coughing lightly, Tatiana fanned the smoke away with her bandaged hand, then she said, "If you'll recall, we had a very hard fight against the Scourge. They were led by Sash. Do you remember him?"

"Of course," Rhonna said.

"Sash was a member of Talon, and needless to say, his methods were very effective but brazen. Not only that, but like Razor, he had a hard time following orders. Eventually, Adanadel and Dalsay kicked him out, but not all agreed," she said. "I personally thought he needed more time and instruction."

"As did I," Tanlin added.

Tatiana continued, "If Sash had remained in our guidance, I believe he would have turned out fine. Instead, he was spurned. That scorn turned to anger. That anger worked against us. I don't want that to happen again."

Rhonna stood up on her chair and said, "You know what the problem with you is? You don't know a bad seed when you see it." She hopped down from the chair. "And wherever I go, they aren't coming with me."

21

The next morning, Zora was outside in the stables, helping Tatiana load up her horse. The mood was as somber as the air was chilly. "I'm sorry, Tatiana. I wish you wouldn't go. Not like this."

"You can come with me." Tatiana's face was drawn tight. She grimaced when she loaded a bedroll onto the back of her saddle and tied it down. "You'd be better off."

"I can't. I need to be with them for Grey Cloak, and I can't let down Dyphestive, either. I'm sorry."

"You don't need to be sorry. You need to be careful." Tatiana patted her cheek. "Listen to me. This is only one step in a long journey. Besides, it's best that I return the dragon charm to the Wizard Watch sooner rather than later. There is a tower northwest of here. That is where I'll go. Perhaps it's for the best."

"I know *I'm* not complaining." Razor was in the next stall, strapping the bastard sword to his horse. He was dressed in full battle gear, decorated with swords and daggers snug in their sheaths along his body. "The last thing I want to do is work for someone that is ungrateful. You risk your neck to save someone, and this is the thanks you get. If you ask me, that dwarf has lost a marble or two." He tapped two fingers to his head. "I'd be careful if I were you."

"I'm sorry to see you and Grunt go," Zora said.

"Believe me, I'll miss that pretty smile and lovely figure." He came closer, grabbed her hand, and kissed it. "Perhaps we'll meet again and I'll show you a good time."

Zora found it difficult to pull her grip free of his. For a moment, he held her captivated with his smiling eyes and warm but cocky grin. "Let's stay friends."

He let go. "Nothing wrong with that. Friendship is the first step to something more." He winked at her and turned away. "Grunt! Quit drinking out of that trough. It's time to go!"

Giving Tatiana one last hug, Zora said, "I'll miss you. Be careful."

"I will," Tatiana replied. "Dragon speed, dear sister. Dragon speed."

22

LOOSE BOOT

The journey north was long, even when flying on a dragon's back. Grey Cloak and Anya rubbed their tired eyes when they landed along the snowcapped mountain ranges of Ice Vale. A heavy snow was falling.

Grey Cloak stood ankle deep in the snow and yawned. Yawning was something that he rarely did, but Cinder had flown nonstop, day and night. Even the grand dragon looked tired as he lay in a snowbank, his eyelids drooping.

Anya handed Grey Cloak a small pack of gear. "Take this. It should tide you over while you wait for your friends. Loose Boot is little more than a league from here, but I wouldn't dally. Once nightfall comes, you'll freeze to death without proper shelter."

"Huh? You aren't coming with me?" he asked absentmindedly as he watched Streak plow his chubby body through the snow. "I thought you would wait with me."

"You might as well ask me to kiss the face of Black Frost himself. We are too close to his territory. I think I've done enough to risk bringing you here. You are on your own now." She nodded. "Best to you and your journey. I hope you find Dyphestive." She turned and walked away.

Something gnawed at his gut. Anya had risked everything for him, and she was walking away. He couldn't let that happen. It didn't seem fair. "Anya, wait! Please."

She stopped.

"Listen, you are in trouble anyway. Why rush off?" He blocked her path. "Come to Loose Boot with me, at least for a little while."

"Why?"

"Well... because."

"'Because' isn't a reason." She stepped forward, practically pushing him out of the way.

"Stay and talk, Anya, only a night. You're tired, you need food, and I think, once our heads clear, perhaps we might find a way to sort matters out."

"What matters are you talking about?"

"You know, matters. For instance, maybe there are other ways to defeat Black Frost that haven't been considered. Maybe he has a weakness. Perhaps the Wizard Watch knows something. I don't know."

"It certainly seems that you *don't know*. You aren't

making any sense," she said as she made her way over to Cinder.

The dragon's eyes were closed, and snow had already built up on his body.

Anya patted Cinder on the horn. "Cinder, it's time to go."

The dragon snored.

"Cinder!" She dusted the snow away from his fist-sized earhole. "Cinder, wake up!"

The grand dragon's snoring continued, and his eyes remained closed.

"Thunderbolts! He's asleep!"

"And that's bad?" Grey Cloak asked.

"Yes, it's bad. The long flight must have exhausted him." She shook her head in disgust. "He's getting old."

Grey Cloak tightened his cloak around his body as the winds picked up, and he brushed his hair away from his eyes. "How long does he need to sleep?"

"It's been a while," she said with a frown. She kicked Cinder. "Thunderbolts, I can't believe he did this. Now, of all times. Unbelievable. What are you smiling at?"

"It looks like you're going to be keeping me company after all."

"Don't think for a moment that I'm going to leave him." She sat down in the snow with an angry look on her face. "I'll stay put."

"It's going to get colder," he said. "Don't worry about

him. The snow will cover him, and he'll look like part of the mountain." He extended his hand to her. "Come on, Anya. Cinder will be fine. Let's go to Loose Boot."

She took his hand and let him pull her up. "One night."

He nodded. "One night it is."

Together, they began the long trek through the deepening snow.

23

Loose Boot was a large and thriving mining and timber community surrounded by great pine and oak trees that stood over a hundred feet tall. The town itself wasn't extraordinary compared to the cities in the south, but it was warm and quaint. Coal-fired urns lit up the corner of every block and outlined the streets. It had blocks and blocks of wood and stone lodges surrounded by miles of smaller cottages in the snowy countryside.

The citizens from all walks of life shuffled by in furs and great coats. There were hunters, trappers, dwarves, halflings, and gnomes. Most of the men wore beards, and the women were bundled up so tight that you could barely see their faces.

Despite the cold, the people were robust, even friendly,

seemingly oblivious to Gapoli's troubles. Hence, the northwest had a nickname called the Great Escape.

After the bitterly cold trek through knee-deep snow in some places, Grey Cloak and Anya settled inside one of many great lodges. Grey Cloak warmed his toes by the fire and sipped on a hot cup of cocoa. Streak nuzzled by the hearth, his scales blending in with the stone. Given his small size, he looked more like a lizard than a dragon, and none of the patrons paid them any mind.

Anya sat at the table, dipping hot bread into a bowl heaped with stew. It was her second bowl.

"I've never seen you eat so much," Grey Cloak said.

"When it's cold, I eat." She looked over her shoulder at the large double-door entry.

The lodge had a huge main floor with several fireplaces. Long tables in the middle stretched from one end of the room to the other. Most of the bench seats were half full.

"It doesn't hurt that it's tasty, either. Aren't you going to eat more?"

Grey Cloak stared into the fire. "I suppose I will in a bit. I'm fine at the moment."

"What's on your mind?"

"I don't know how long I'll need to wait. It hasn't been a year as of yet." He picked up a fire poker and moved the logs in the crackling fire. "And I'm not well suited for sitting around and wasting time."

A timber wolf, one of many in the lodge, wandered toward the fireplace with its ice-blue eyes on Streak. The hackles on its white-and-black fur were raised. It poked its black nose at Streak and sniffed.

Streak's eyelids remained shut. He was curled up in a tight ball.

"Easy, wolf," Grey Cloak said.

The wolf sniffed Streak from head to tail. It licked Streak's body, pulled back, bared its teeth, and growled.

"Jock, down!" someone with a commanding voice said. A big, bearded man covered in bear furs lumbered between the tables and smacked the wolf on the head. "Get out of here, Jock!" He set his eyes on Grey Cloak and Anya. "Apologies. My wolf can be nosy." He squatted and tilted his head as his gaze landed on Streak. "I'll be. That's a runt dragon, is it not?"

Grey Cloak nodded. "Only a fool would bring the real thing in here."

"Hah, you'd be surprised what we get in these parts. All sorts. All sorts." The man's voice was strong and cheerful. "I'm Archibald West, but you can call me Archi." He extended his meaty, calloused hand. "I'm a lumberjack."

"It's nice to meet you, Archi." Grey Cloak shook his hand. Archi had a grip of steel.

After shaking Anya's hand, Archi sat down beside her. "You've a strong grip for a lady. Ever swing a wood axe before?"

"I've chopped down a few trees in my days. They make excellent firewood."

"Ha!" Archi slapped his knee. "Listen, if you want the really good eatin', try the trout. The streams in these parts are full of them." He parted his hands wide. "They are this big and delicious."

"What makes you think we're new to the territory?" Anya asked.

"Oh, no offense, but I can tell. I've lived here all my life, and I take it upon myself to meet people." He touched his finger to his hawklike nose. "Yeah, I'm nosy. And I'm not the only one. But don't feel uncomfortable. Loose Boot is a fine place, a fine place for two young lovebirds to get away."

Anya dropped her spoon. "What? We are no such thing. Only friends."

"Maybe you are his protector then," Archi said as he eyed the metal bracers over her armor.

She covered it up with her cloak and put her hands underneath the table. "If you would excuse us, Archibald, we would like to enjoy our meal in peace."

"Fine, fine." He stood up. "I apologize for my pushy behavior. It's how I am. Only trying to be friendly." He winked at her and rubbed Grey Cloak's shoulder. "I'll leave you two lovebirds alone. But if you need anything, anything at all, just ask for Archi." He made his way through the rows of benches, patting shoulders and greeting everyone he passed.

"What do you make of him?" Grey Cloak asked.

Anya watched the bear of a man disappear through the front doors with his wolf in tow. "I think we'd better keep an eye on him, because he's definitely got his eye on us."

24

DARK MOUNTAIN

Led by Drysis, the Doom Riders, including the new member, Iron Bones, passed through the main gate, known as the Iron Curtain, and made their way down the Long Road into the bitter wasteland called Ugrad. The Brothers of Destruction were riding on their gourn, fearsome dragon horses, and turning even the most daring stares away.

All of the men were wearing their leather skull-like masks dyed in dreary colors. Scar's was crimson, Shamrok's was green, Ghost's was blue, and Iron Bones's was black. Their suits of leather armor were fashioned like dragon scales. Even the Black Guard found it difficult to look upon them with anything but fear and awe.

Drysis, though a woman, sat as tall in the saddle as any man. Her rotating crossbow hung behind her wide shoulders. Her face was set in a scowl. As they passed under the Iron Curtain, she looked over her shoulder at her men and nodded. The gourn she was riding reared, and the other four did the same. Then they spewed flames from their mouths and upward into the night sky.

The Black Guard, known as the Terror Troops, came to life with roaring cheers. The gourn dropped down on all fours, smoke streaming from their nostrils. As one, they lunged forward and thundered down the Long Road.

"I love doing that!" Shamrok shouted. "Some of them worship us like Riskers!"

"In your dreams," Scar yelled back. "As for me, I'm hungry for the open trail and the wind at my back. It's time to raid the taverns of commoners and do some hunting." His grip tightened on his reins. "Eeyah!"

The Doom Riders rode all night, trampling surprised critters and people that crossed their paths on more than one occasion. They did not stop until the sun came over the mountaintops and shone on their faces. Navigating through the icy tundra's tall grasses, they slowed to a trot.

Iron Bones had not said a word since they departed. Behind his mask, his eyes absorbed everything he passed. Everything was new to him but, in an odd way, vaguely familiar. He didn't know what to make of it.

The company dismounted by a stream that bordered a leafless forest. Drysis dipped her canteen into the water and drank a palmful from her hand.

Shamrok did the same and said, "I take it that you know where we're going?"

"Of course."

He plugged the cap on his canteen. "Care to share?"

She hung her canteen over her shoulder and said, "Word has it that some halfling villages are harboring Black Frost's enemies. We are going to pay them a visit."

Shamrok grinned. "A halfling breakfast. It's been a while."

"It's not you that I want to see feast, but him." She looked at Iron Bones.

He'd remained in the saddle, listening to every word while watching a pair of chipmunks scramble up the branches of what appeared to be dead trees.

"Iron Bones!" Drysis said.

He turned his stare slowly toward her. "Yes, Mother?"

"It has been a long time since you last saw action." She walked to him. "How is your head?"

"Fine," he replied in a voice devoid of emotion.

"Are you ready to destroy our enemies?"

"I am ready to destroy everything."

Scar cursed under his breath and made it sound like a sneeze.

Drysis glared at the man, but he shrugged. She lifted her eyes to Iron Bones and said, "Your mother is looking forward to seeing you in action soon." She put her hand on his thigh. "Think of it as a new beginning for you and me—for all of us."

He nodded.

A HALFLING VILLAGE was well concealed in a valley between two of Ugrad's rocky hills. The robust people, slight in build and strong in work ethic, moved quickly from hut to hut, storehouse to storehouse, and barn to barn. They fed the livestock, cranked water out of the wells, and churned butter.

The durable men smoked pipes. The women wore bonnets and had their hair in pigtails. They were lively in spirit and character and ready for any challenge that met them.

From a distance, the Doom Riders watched them.

Drysis was knee to knee with Iron Bones. "Are you ready?" she asked.

"What is your wish, Mother?"

"Take your gourn. Ride down there and kill them all."

Iron Bones looked away from her and down at the field of little people. He flicked his gourn's reins and said, "As you wish, Mother."

Scar and Shamrok flanked Drysis.

"Are you sure you don't want us to go down there with him?" Shamrok asked. "That's a lot of halflings."

"No worries. We'll track down any runaways," she said.

"Not that I have any affection for halflings—for the most part, I think they are worthless," Scar said. "But why them? They don't pose a challenge for the likes of us or him. Are they truly traitors?"

"Perhaps. Who knows the heart of anyone? But this isn't about them. It's about him." She eyed Iron Bones, who was slowly leading his horse down the rugged hill. "He won't truly be one of us until his hands are stained with innocent blood. Besides, no one is going to miss a halfling."

25

Zora held her stomach and looked away from the carnage. The smoke in the air made her eyes water, and her nose burned from the stench of charred flesh. "Who could do such a thing?" she asked, almost choking on the words.

Rhonna walked through the halfling village, surveying while rolling her cigar from one side of her mouth to the other.

It looked like a tornado of death had struck the hardy people. Panic-stricken faces were mixed with dead eyes frozen in horror—the ones that weren't burned were mutilated.

Zora swallowed the lump in her throat when Rhonna answered her question. "Doom Riders."

"This is awful," Tanlin said, holding his scarf over his

mouth. "Who kills halflings? They are the least threatening people."

"Doom Riders," Rhonna said again.

"It was a rhetorical question."

Lythlenion scoured the grounds, searching for survivors requiring aid.

Bowbreaker was down on one knee with his hand on the ground. "I've only found one set of gourn prints and one man's footprints in the village. This man is a heavy man. Heavier than most."

"They wear armor," Tanlin commented.

Bowbreaker nodded and rose, lifting his gaze to the hill that overlooked the valley village. "He came from the top. The others watched."

"Where did they go?" Rhonna asked.

"South."

Talon had been tracking the Doom Riders since they departed from the Long Road of Dark Mountain but hadn't come within a day's ride of the vicious warriors. Bowbreaker had tracked them, taking his time, careful not to let them know that anyone was on their trail, then they'd waited a day before they approached the halfling village, making sure the way was clear. It would take patience to learn the methods of the Doom Riders and figure out a way to rescue Dyphestive.

Zora approached Bowbreaker and said, "You said that one rider did all of this?"

He shook his head. "No. The halfling men fought. The women and children ran and hid. I believe the others, the watchers on the hill, took them out."

"You don't think it was Dyphestive, do you?" Zora said. "He killed all of these men?"

"I don't know the youth," Bowbreaker replied.

"Zora, are you sure that Dyphestive was in the right state of mind when you met with him?" Tanlin asked.

"Absolutely. He was himself, little different from the day I met him. He was glum at first but filled with hope the moment he saw me and learned about Grey Cloak." She looked away from two charred bodies that caught her eye. "He'd never do this. Perhaps it is not him that is with them."

"I caught a look at him from a distance when they departed. And I'd know Dyphestive's barn build anywhere. Even though he had a mask on, I knew it was him," Rhonna said.

Zora's shoulders sagged.

"Over here," Lythlenion called. He was lifting the roof of a hut that had burned and collapsed. "I heard someone coughing."

Bowbreaker helped him lift what was left of the roof and cast it aside. An elderly halfling was balled up in the fetal position on the ground, shivering like a leaf and squeezing his eyes shut.

"He's half frozen to death," Lythlenion said as he picked

up the small man in tattered clothing. "Make a fire and fetch him a cloak or a blanket if you can find one."

Zora scrounged up a blanket from the burning wreckage and covered the halfling with it.

The old halfling had a head full of cotton-white hair and sideburns. He shook uncontrollably and began to mutter. "Please don't kill me. Please don't kill me."

Lythlenion bundled the man up like a baby and said, "No one is going to hurt you. The danger is gone. Open your eyes, and you'll see friendly faces."

"No, no," the old man muttered.

"He's still frightened," Lythlenion said to the others. "Give me some time with him." He fished in his pouches and produced some nuts and dried beef. "Will you eat? You must be hungry."

The old halfling sniffed. "I smell meat. Burning meat! No, no, nooo!" he wailed.

"We have to get him away from this place." Lythlenion picked up the halfling. "Come on." He moved away from the village, out of sight of the carnage and upwind from the stench. Among the rocks in the hills, they made another fire.

It took over an hour for the halfling's trembling to stop. When it did, he opened his eyes and drank from Lythlenion's canteen. "They are all dead, aren't they?" the halfling asked.

"I'm sorry, but you are the only survivor that we've found so far. My name is Lythlenion. What is yours?"

"It doesn't matter now." The halfling rocked back and forth. He took fleeting glances at the other members of the company. "I was the oldest. I should have died, not the youngest. Now our people have no legacy."

Zora sat down beside the halfling and asked, "How many of you were there?"

"Twenty-one," he said with a sniffle. "They were all my family."

The halfling's words pierced Zora's heart as she saw visions of Deeann and her pack of halflings. Her chest tightened at the thought that it could have been them. "I'm sorry to ask, but did you see what happened?"

"I saw him," the old halfling said. "I saw death. He rode in on his dragon horse and trampled my family." His soft eyes widened. "Flames gushed out of the beast's mouth, setting the huts aflame. It killed without discernment. He killed in spite of the cries of mercy. I tried to warn them, but it was too late. My family panicked." His chin dipped. "The women tried to save the children. The men tried to save the women. Many of them stood up to put up a fight." He suddenly shook. "Death killed them."

"What did death look like?" she asked.

"He was built like an ox and wore a terrible black mask." The halfling blinked the tears from his eyes. His next words were haunting. "I saw death, and it was him."

26

Talon spent the entire day burying the dead, or at least what was left of them. In many cases, the gourn's flames had incinerated the innocent halflings. The hardest part was burying the children. Their trampled bodies were broken. The halfling women had hidden them all in a nearby burrow for safety, but the Doom Riders had flushed them out and killed them.

Zora heaved a shovelful of dirt into a shallow grave. Her lower back was as tight as a bowstring, her arms taut from the grueling hours of labor, but she wouldn't stop. She was numb.

Lythlenion stood beside her, leaning on his shovel and wiping the sweat from his brow. The usually cheerful orc's face was expressionless. "Why don't you rest, Zora?"

"I can't. Besides, these graves will need markers." She

patted the hump of loose dirt with her shovel. "I'll need to work on that once this is over."

Rhonna was nearby, and so was Tanlin. Everyone was soaked in sweat, and the lowering sun was shining in their eyes. The only one that wasn't present was Bowbreaker. He was tracking the Doom Riders.

Since they'd started digging, Rhonna hadn't said a word. Her silence seemed to suggest that she was more saddened than the others. It was she who knew Dyphestive best. She'd all but raised him.

The old halfling had finally offered his name as Cotton, saying that he'd been called that all of his life because his hair was so curly and white. Weeping loudly from time to time, he'd piled up whatever possessions that had worth and hadn't been destroyed. His sobs brought new tears to Zora's eyes every time.

"You've been very quiet, Rhonna. Do you care to share what is on your mind?" Tanlin asked.

"No," Rhonna replied.

"I will then." Tanlin stopped shoveling. "As fond as I am of Dyphestive, we need to consider the possibility that he is lost."

"How can you say that?" Zora practically spit the words out. "What do you mean?"

Tanlin laid down his shovel and said in a sympathetic tone, "Zora, as much as I hate to say it, perhaps it's too late to save him. Dyphestive might have changed forever. He killed innocent halflings. The act itself is abominable." He scanned the surprised looks on everyone's faces. "I don't think I'm alone in saying that any one of us would rather die than commit such an act."

"You can't know that, Tanlin! We don't know what has happened to him," she said. "I can't believe you of all people would say that."

"Zora, my point is that we all might be risking our necks for a lost cause. All of us could die, and for what? To try to save a young man that is beyond saving?"

With downcast eyes, they all stood silent.

"Aren't any of you going to disagree with him?" Zora's voice cracked. "Anyone?"

"He makes a good point," Rhonna said.

Zora's jaw dropped. "How dare you? He is your friend!" She threw her shovel at Rhonna.

Rhonna deftly sidestepped it, glowered at Zora, and said, "I said he made a good point! I didn't say that I agreed! Settle yourself, girl, or I'll turn you over my knee."

Zora stiffened. "Humph!"

"Listen to me. All of you. No one is giving up on Dyphestive. Yes, this deed is an atrocity, but the young man I know would never do such a thing. But we have to consider the possibility that he's changed. That he's gone. None of us knows what sort of evil could have caught ahold of him, but it's not something that I haven't seen before." She glanced at Lythlenion, who nodded. "Any one of us can be deceived, but I also know that any one of us can be saved. We came to Ugrad to find out if he is still alive. He is. And if he can be saved, we'll save him, no matter what the cost."

Zora rushed over and hugged her. "I'm sorry I threw a shovel at you."

"Don't let it happen again. And quit hugging me." Rhonna gently broke free of Zora's embrace and took out a cigar. "As much as I hate to admit it, Grey Cloak was right. We should have gotten Dyphestive out of there as fast as we could. Now, it looks like the damage is done. That doesn't mean it can't be undone, but it will be hard."

"What are we going to do?" Tanlin asked. "If Dyphestive has become a Doom Rider, he'll try to kill us. How are we supposed to save a man that wants to kill us? Not to mention we have three more Doom Riders and Drysis to contend with."

Rhonna rolled her cigar from one side of her mouth to the other. "I've known Drysis a long time. She was raised in Dark Mountain but fought alongside the Monarchs. She has her shortcomings, like being overconfident. We'll have to use that against her."

"What are you suggesting?"

"I don't have the details sorted out, but we're going to have to get ahead of them. Separate Dyphestive from the pack." She rubbed her strong chin. "The location will be key. The planning will have to be precise. The execution, perfect."

"I'll do whatever I can to help," Zora said.

"We all will, of course," Tanlin added.

"You're an excellent planner, Rhonna. I look forward to seeing what you come up with," Lythlenion said.

"It will take a lot of teamwork," Rhonna replied. "But we'll find a way to do it."

"What about me?" Cotton asked quietly. He'd eased his way into their midst. "I have nothing. Nowhere to go, no family, but I'd like to help. We halflings might be small, but we can still be vengeful."

"This isn't about vengeance," Rhonna said. "It's about saving our friend."

"Yes, your friend that killed my family," Cotton replied woefully.

"We aren't trying to kill him. I don't think you understand that."

"No, I do. We halflings have a saying: 'A rotten apple offers the best fertilizer.'"

The company exchanged doubtful looks.

"That's not a very good saying," Lythlenion said.

"It is halfling wisdom. You wouldn't understand it. Regardless, I will look this Dyphestive in the eye. If he can be saved, I will know." Cotton picked up a stick that had a sack tied to the end. "I'm ready."

27

LOOSE BOOT

Grey Cloak and Anya walked through the snow-covered streets of Loose Boot. Timbermen drove sleighs down the snow-packed roads, hauling sleds of lumber. Gnomes wearing knit caps were busy shoveling the snow from their porches. Every building had a chimney or two that was smoking.

"Do you think you could ever live in such a place?" Grey Cloak asked. He had Streak lying over his shoulders. The dragon's wagging tail kept hitting him in the face. He pushed it away. "Will you stop that?"

"Dragons have minds of their own, don't you know," Anya said.

"Yes, I can feel that."

"As for the north, I don't care for it. I like a warmer climate."

"I think I would be bored." He ducked away from a snowball, which flew over his head. Many children were battling along the streets. "It looks like there is nothing to do here but work, eat, and make babies. Speaking of babies, aren't you at that child-bearing age where you should be making some?"

Anya's face lit up with disgust. "I'm not some milk maiden. I'm a Sky Rider."

"Back in Havenstock, you'd be called an old maid. I mean, shouldn't you be getting married by now?"

"I'm not that old."

"You're much older than I am. You don't want to wait around until the cupboard is barren, do you?"

She punched him in the shoulder. "Stifle it!"

"Or what?"

"I'll stick a thunder javelin down your throat."

He erupted in laughter, smirked, and said, "If only you had one. Come now, don't frown. You can't tell me that you don't think about it. Or are you strictly married to vengeance?"

"I'm not married to anyone. Not anyone at all. The truth is, I've never had much time to think of it," she said. "And I don't want to think about it now." She pushed him away. A snowball hit her square in the face. "Aaargh! You little rodents!"

She and Grey Cloak started making snowballs and hurling them at the children. The battle with the gleefully giggling children crisscrossed through the streets. All of a sudden, it seemed like every child in Loose Boot was attacking. They were getting pelted from all directions. They dashed away and hid behind a wagon.

"Are you certain that you don't want to be a mother?" he asked as he flung a snowball, which exploded in an orc boy's face.

"I'm more certain now than ever! They are heathens!" Anya unleashed three snowballs without discrimination. The shots blasted two girls and one boy square in the face. "Come on!"

They dashed down an alley, navigated the side streets, and emerged in another section of Loose Boot that didn't have any children around.

As they leaned against an alley wall, Anya caught her breath. "Thanks to them, I'm even less inclined to get married than I was yesterday."

"Hah, so you *have* been thinking about it?"

"Hardly." She moved into the main street. "Judging by all of the hammering that I can hear, I think we're in the laborers' district. Probably won't see any children around here. They'd put them to work."

Grey Cloak dusted the snow from his cloak and spied a familiar building. "It can't be..."

"What can't be?"

Wedged in an alley, between the stone buildings, was a rickety wooden hovel three stories tall. A sign on a chain hung over the porch front. Grey Cloak stood under it with his eyes fixed on the red lettering.

"Batram's Bartery and Arcania?" Anya asked. "What of it?"

He smirked. "It can't be the same store," he muttered as he recalled the store in Raven Cliff that magically came and went. "Or could it?" He took the stairs onto the porch and stood before a huge red door. "Huh, the door used to be black, but I swear it's the same store." He smirked. "It has to be."

"What are you doing? You aren't going in there, are you?"

He grabbed her wrist and said, "Yes, and you are coming too."

The red door swung wide open. A brisk wind seemingly pushed them inside, and the door slammed shut behind them.

"Welcome!" someone with a coarse but familiar voice said. "Wipe your feet!"

With eyes widening, Anya asked, "Is this rug talking?"

"Yes," Grey Cloak said as he wiped his feet on the pelt of a razorback boar that still had its head attached.

"Ah," the boar moaned with pleasure. "That feels very good!"

Anya hesitantly wiped her feet and stepped toward the front counter. She lifted her eyes to the tall rows of wooden shelving, which rose over thirty feet in the air. "This building from the outside doesn't look that tall at all." She stared down the rows of shelving behind the counter. "Or deep."

"It's a strange place," Grey Cloak said, his own eyes widening.

Batram's Bartery and Arcania was an exact replica of the store that he remembered. The glass countertop was framed in polished dark mahogany. The chestnut shelving on the other side started with coffin-sized storage drawers at the bottom and ended with the smallest drawers at the top. The fittings were aged solid brass. The floorboards creaked.

"You've been here before?" she asked, her eyes fixed on the items displayed inside the counter. It had swords, daggers, bracers, gauntlets, arrows, potion vials, broaches, and rings. "These are fantastic things."

"Haven't you ever gone shopping?'"

"No." Anya lifted her eyes and immediately pulled her sword.

A towering humanoid with the head of a spider, eight human arms, and two human legs emerged from behind the counter and stood before them. He was wearing a white-and-red-striped vest with a yellow carnation in the upper pocket. He spread his arms out wide. "I am Batram. Welcome to my arcania."

28

"That's a fine sword," Batram said, his bug eyes blinking. He tilted his towering body to one side and stooped down a bit. "A sky blade, is it not?"

Anya moved backward with a repulsed look on her face. "Grey Cloak, what is this thing?"

"I'm no thing," Batram said defensively.

"He's no thing. He's a halfling—at least, I think he is," Grey Cloak replied. He petted Streak, who was on his shoulders. The dragon slipped into his hood and nestled.

Anya stepped back farther. "That doesn't look like a halfling." The back of her bootheel stepped on the skin of the razorback boar.

"Welcome!" the rug said. "Be sure to wipe your feet... please."

"Oh, stifle it!" Anya said to the rug with a backward glance.

"May I look at your sword?" Batram said. "It's been a long time since I've handled a sky blade."

"No," she said as she turned back around. "Dragons of deception! How did he do that?"

Batram was standing on top of the counter as a full-sized halfling. He only had two arms and two legs but was still wearing his striped vest. His hair was curly and a mix of white and red. He wiggled his caterpillar eyebrows when he spoke. "Do what, my dear?"

"You know what. Come, Grey Cloak, we are getting out of here," she ordered.

Grey Cloak raised his hands, palms upward, and said, "He does that. You'll get used to it, I think."

"Yes, Sky Rider, please stay. As you've heard, you are welcome." Batram's eyes had a friendly glint in them. "You sound like some sort of barbarian that is spooked by simple magic."

"This doesn't look so simple," she said as she eased her sword back into its sheath and looked around the arcania. "What is this place?"

Batram scratched his wooly sideburns. "I always found the sheltered lives of the Sky Riders to be fascinating." He paced along the counter. "They keep so close to their own that one rarely crosses them. I delight in a mind-expanding moment like this."

"Sheltered." Grey Cloak smirked as he eyed her.

"I'm not sheltered. Sky Riders don't embrace or indulge in the vices of the common world. We focus on a loftier way of living."

"Such as living for vengeance," he joked.

With her nose turned up, she said, "Someone has to fight the good fight. We certainly aren't going to stand around and do nothing while evil tightens its grip on the world. We have our gifts. It would be without purpose not to use them."

"A well-stated point," Batram said. "I agree." He walked to the end of his counter and stopped where the shelving bumped into it. He opened up a wooden drawer just above his head. On tiptoe, he reached in the drawer and pulled out a dagger. "I suppose this is what you came for?"

Grey Cloak gaped. It was the dagger that he'd stolen from the gnoll at Farhook, near the Iron Hills, when he and Dyphestive were rescuing their sheep. The dagger was well crafted, almost a foot long, with a black blade and a wooden handle. He moved toward it. So much had happened since the first time he met Batram that he'd forgotten all about it.

"I'm good to my word. I told you I would get it back," Batram said. "I'll take the cloak back, and you can have the dagger in return. That is our agreement."

With his eyes glued to the dagger, Grey Cloak said absentmindedly, "What?"

Batram extended the dagger, which might as well have been a sword in his little hands.

Grey Cloak eased back and tightened his cloak around his neck. "I think that we should leave things where they are. I've become very fond of this cloak." He patted his hip. "And I have another dagger."

Batram's eyebrows wiggled. "Don't be a donkey skull. This is a hard-tooth dagger. It will pierce through stone and the finest armor." He spun the dagger over and tossed it from one hand to the other. "It's perfectly balanced. Any warrior would cherish it."

"Not interested." He rustled his cloak like a cape made of bird feathers. "I've grown to be very fond of this *old* garb."

"Don't be foolish. Take the dagger," Anya said. She reached for him. "Take it off."

"No. I like the cloak."

Batram plopped down on the counter and kicked his little legs over the edge. "Fascinating. You really are fond of that cloak, but it has no discernible powers that I detected." He jammed the dagger in the countertop. "Tell me about the cloak."

Grey Cloak moved away from Batram's piercing gaze. "It's as you said. It keeps me warm and the rain off my back. What more could an elf ask for?"

"It does more than that, doesn't it?" Batram said.

"No," Grey Cloak said with his eyes averted. He looked

into the display glass, which had a large metal gauntlet with gemstones set in the knuckles. "That's interesting. What is it?"

Batram hopped to his feet. His face was red with fury. He turned instantly into the eight-armed bug man and thrust four of his right index fingers at Grey Cloak. "You're hiding something! What is it?"

29

Anya whisked her sky blade out. "Back away, Batram, or I'll cut you open like a melon."

"Don't toy with me!" Batram leaned over the counter. With a wave of his left hands, Anya's sword ripped free of her grasp and stuck in the adjacent wall. His many arms reached for Grey Cloak.

The arcania's foyer was a tight space, leaving little room for Grey Cloak to maneuver. He ducked away from Batram's clutches and jumped on the rug.

"Welcome!" the boar's head said. "Please wipe your feet!"

Grey Cloak tugged at the door's handle. It was locked. "Batram, I believe my business here is concluded. I would like to leave."

Batram's arms stretched out like tentacles and snatched

up Grey Cloak by his feet, but Grey Cloak was able to keep his hold on the door handle.

Anya gasped and ran to the wall and pulled her sword free. "Let him go!"

Batram spit a glob of webbing from his mouth, pinning her to the wall.

Holding onto the handle with all of his might, Grey Cloak said, "Batram! This is no way to treat your customers. I'll spread word if you don't unhand me now!" His grip was ripped free from the handle. "Aaah!"

Batram dangled Grey Cloak upside down. "You are a troublesome elf. Be truthful with me." He started shaking Grey Cloak up and down. "What powers has this cloak concealed?"

"I don't know what you're talking about!"

"You dare treat me like a fool?" Batram had a voice like thunder. "Answer me now." He shook Grey Cloak harder and harder.

"Stop it, you monstrosity!" Anya cried. She was stuck to the wall like a fly in a web. Her wriggling tightened the strands of webbing around her. "Let me go!"

Coins and small gemstones fell from Grey Cloak's pockets and bounced on the counter.

Batram's eyes widened. "What's this?" His tentacles rummaged through Grey Cloak's secret pockets. "I don't recall this cloak having any pockets." They dug deeper into the inner folds of the cloak.

"Stop it!" Grey Cloak demanded.

"Why?"

"It tickles." It didn't really, but he couldn't think of anything else to say. Whatever Batram was, he was powerful. His tentacles were as strong as iron and impossible to break. "Please, put me down, Batram. I haven't done anything wrong."

"What's this?" Batram removed the Figurine of Heroes and gazed at it.

Grey Cloak snatched at the figurine. "That's mine! A gift from a friend."

"I know this," Batram said in a hushed voice. "The Figurine of Heroes. How did you come to possess it?"

With his hair dangling over the counter, Grey Cloak crossed his arms and replied, "Put me down."

"No. You are in my bartery, and I have all of the power here. Tell me!" Batram shook him hard. "Tell me now!"

"Tell him, Grey Cloak, so we can get out of here," Anya said.

"No."

"We have more important matters to attend to," she added.

He rolled his eyes. "Fine. A wizard of the watch, Dalsay, possessed it. He died, and I came upon it."

"I see." Batram's bug eyes studied the figurine. It was solid onyx carved in the shape of a faceless person. "And the cloak. What of it?"

Grey Cloak sighed. "If you must know, it has many pockets that, well, move."

Batram arched an eyebrow. "And?"

"And... it floats."

"Floats? Like a duck?"

"More like a leaf, falling from the sky."

"I'll be. I'll be."

Batram released Grey Cloak. He swayed as if he'd seen a ghost.

"All this time."

Grey Cloak hunkered down on the counter with worried eyes fixed on Batram. He glanced at Anya, who twisted in her webbing, and shrugged. "'All this time' what?"

Batram's fiery temperament had softened a great deal. He ran his top two tentacle hands over the cloak's shoulders and downward. "My fingertips know the touch of magic. That is what I do. That is why I am. But in this garment, I sense no magic at all, yet I see it for myself. Though I might feel it, I know that this is. I am a historian of marvels. But I never believed it still existed."

"You know what this is," Grey Cloak said as he spread out the folds of his cloak.

The room lit up with a flash of white light. Anya fell free from her bonds and stood with her sword out. The sky blade glowed with fire. "Spit on me again, and I'll run you through, bug troll!"

"I'm neither a bug nor a troll. I was beginning to wonder if you had the smarts to use your wizardry," Batram said. He'd assumed the form of a halfling again. "And you are very temperamental."

"That's only a taste of it," Grey Cloak said. "Now tell me about my cloak."

Batram rubbed his jaw and said, "I can't be certain, but I believe that it is the Cloak of Legends. Its power will only be revealed to the person that can use it... or the person that it chooses, rather."

"You speak like it's a living thing."

"All magic has life, the same as you, me, plants, and animals. We are all part of it. But this cloak was made with a purpose. Woven by sorcerers and wizards that this world has long forgotten. If I could only use it." He tightened his fingers around the figurine. "This bauble should be suitable payment for it."

"No, that's my figurine."

"Then give me the cloak back."

"It is not of any use to you or anyone. Besides, the cloak chose me."

"A fair trade is a fair trade." Batram cradled the cloak to his chest. "The Cloak of Legends contains many wonders. You are very blessed to have it. Please take your leave." He waved his hand, and the door flew open. The cold northern air blew in. "Now!"

"Go, go, go," Batram said as he flicked his hands at them. "Before I turn back into my big self." His face transformed into a tarantula head. "Don't make me say it again!"

"I'm not leaving without my figurine. Besides, you can't use it if you don't know the words of summoning," Grey Cloak said.

Batram eyed the figurine. "I'll figure it out. I know people. Ouch!"

Streak had snuck out of Grey Cloak's hood and onto the counter and bitten Batram on his bare toe. The halfling dropped the figurine.

In the wink of an eye, Grey Cloak snatched the figurine out of the air. "Run, Anya!" He scooped up Streak and dashed for the closing door.

"Come back here!" Batram hollered as he hopped up and down, holding his foot. "Come back here now!"

Anya slipped through the closing door. Grey Cloak knifed through the diminishing crack, slid over the icy porch and off the steps, and landed in the snow. The door slammed shut.

He scrambled to his feet and looked at Anya, who was standing in front of the door. "Run!" he said.

"Why?"

He raced up the steps and shoved her down the wooden walkway just as the door burst back open and giant spider legs came out. They were covered in coarse black hair. They probed the porch posts and planks and stretched out into the snow-covered street.

Grey Cloak shoved Anya in the back and pushed her along until the shock had worn off enough for her to run on her own. Both of them sprinted away from Batram's Bartery and Arcania and didn't stop until the building was far out of sight. They ducked into an alley and stopped, panting.

Holding her belly, Anya said, "You spend time in very strange places."

"I suppose I do."

"How'd you stumble upon him anyway, or should I ask?"

"It's a long story." He held Streak up before him.

The chubby, flat-headed dragon looked at him with dead eyes. His pink tongue flicked out of his mouth.

"Well done, Streak. I have my figure back thanks to you," he said cheerfully.

"That's not all that you have," Anya said. She held up the hard-tooth dagger and smiled.

"Why, you little thief!"

"I'm not a thief. I thought it was yours," she said as she tried to hand it to him. "I thought Batram took it from you."

"I pawned it for money. When I got the money back to pay him, he'd sold it. He gave me the cloak in return." Grey Cloak scratched his head. "We are even, the way I see it, but not with the dagger. That's still his collateral. We need to take it back."

"Are you mad? I'm not going back there."

He took the dagger. "Maybe not, but I am."

BATRAM SAT on his counter with his legs dangling over the side. He was once again in halfling form and smoking a curled chestnut pipe. Sweet cherry smoke lingered in the air as he eyed his front door.

"The girl stole the dagger," the boar's-head rug said.

"Yes, I'm fully aware of that," Batram replied.

"You lost the Cloak of Legends and the Figurine of Heroes."

Batram cast his gaze down at the rug. "You don't miss anything from your poor vantage point, do you?"

"I don't have anything better to do. So... what are you going to do?"

"About what?"

"Retrieving those items."

"Those items are in the right hands. All but one." He puffed out smoke that took the shape of a dragon. He kept his eyes on the door and waited.

The boar's-head rug eyed the door. "What are you waiting for? Don't you have business in Monarch City?"

Something made a hollow *thuk* on the other side of the red door.

"That is what I was waiting for." Batram waved a hand. The door swung inward. The hard-tooth dagger was stuck in it with a note and a purse of coins attached. He hopped down to the floor, ambled over to the door, took the dagger and the note in hand, and read it out loud. "'We are even.'"

Batram peered outside and scanned the empty snow-covered streets. "No, we are not even, Grey Cloak." He crumpled up the note in his fist. "You owe me." He walked back inside, and the door slammed closed behind him. "The entire world owes me."

GREY CLOAK and Anya made their way back toward the lodge. She was fighting back a smile.

"What is it?" he asked.

Her mouth tightened. "Nothing."

"Come now, you are about to smile about something. Out with it."

"Well, I'll give you credit. You certainly know how to show me a good time."

He walked backward, facing her, and said, "Oh, having a good time, are you?"

She nodded. "The truth is that I don't get out that much, and I'm finding the change of scenery rather... enjoyable."

"Not everyone that isn't a Sky Rider is so bad."

"That's not what I meant," she said, a bit shamefaced. "I suppose I have been sheltered all of my life. The truth is, I'm probably not the best when it comes to dealing with other people. I tend to look down on them."

"You only have to get to know them. I like them, personally. I find them entertaining. Maybe now you can understand why I don't think I'm ready to be a Sky Rider." He spun around with his hands high in the air. "I want to live like this. Free. Free to go, see, and do as I choose."

"The Sky Riders have a saying," she said. "'There is a price for freedom. That price is blood.'"

"And I say, 'What good is having freedom if you can't enjoy it?'"

"Well—"

"Fire! Fire! Fire!" People called from deep in the heart of Loose Boot.

Grey Cloak and Anya ran down the street. A building was being consumed by fire that sent up plumes of white smoke.

A chain of people lined up, feeding buckets of snow to one another to douse the fire.

"We'd better help," Anya said as she went into action and joined the human chain.

People ran from all directions with their arms, buckets, and shovels full of snow and heaved them at the flames. Grey Cloak was caught up in the charging crowd, which was moving at a frenzied pace. A bearish group of men in furs barreled down the road, carrying blocks of ice. People pushed and shoved, and he was knocked around by the husky brutes. He finally spun his way out of the crowd and lent a hand in another chain of people.

The building burned to a crisp, but the spread of the fire was stopped, preventing damage to the other structures as walls of snow were built around it. Streams of melted snow ran under people's feet and began to ice over and freeze.

Grey Cloak caught up with Anya. Many of the citizens were patting her on the back and thanking her, and women hugged her. She stood out among them, taller than average, and imposing but in a good way.

"What a night!" she said.

"You can say that again. We'd better get back to the lodge before we come across any more trouble." He patted himself down and checked his hood. "Streak?"

The dragon typically nestled in his hood, but it was empty.

Grey Cloak took off his hood and rummaged through it. He looked at Anya and said with his voice full of panic, "He's gone. He's gone!"

31

G rey Cloak scoured the area like a madman, calling for his dragon. "Streak! Streak!"

Anya hooked his arm and pulled him aside. "Stop making a fool of yourself and listen to me. Streak would not abandon you. Something more sinister is afoot."

"You think Batram did it?" he asked.

"Of course, who else?"

He shook his head. "I don't think it was him. And I can't say for certain, but I have the impression that he can't leave his building."

"You can't lose your dragon, Grey Cloak," she said. "You can't." She took him by the wrist and headed back toward Batram's Bartery and Arcania.

He twisted away from her and said, "I get the idea." He

ran the rest of the way, and when he got there, Batram's store was gone.

"How in the world did that happen?" Anya asked with astonishment.

"He does that. That's why I don't think he can leave."

Grey Cloak made his way down the alley but didn't find a single scrap of evidence that the building was ever there. He picked up a crumpled-up piece of paper from the ground. It was the note that he'd written to Batram that read "We are even."

"I told you, it wasn't him. He was gone before that fire started."

"If not him, then who?"

Grey Cloak and Anya searched in all directions from the area where the fire was. There wasn't a single dragon paw print to be found anywhere. After hours of searching, they headed back to the lodge. He had a gnawing feeling in his stomach.

Staring glumly into the fire, he said, "I feel sick."

Anya put a reassuring hand on his arm and said, "We'll find him."

"He's only a baby."

"Dragons aren't like people. They grow really fast. Yes,

he is young, but he's intelligent. One way or the other, he will find his way back to you or..."

"Say it... please."

"Or he'll die trying."

His heart ached. "I wish you hadn't said it. How could I have been so foolish? Someone just snatched him from my hood?"

"It does sound unlikely. Unless someone had eyes on you already."

Grey Cloak scanned the room. Even though it was the wee hours of the morning, plenty of people were sitting at the long rows of tables, eating and drinking. Most of them were gossiping about the fire. He caught Archibald West's eye. The grizzly of a man was with a small group of men. He nodded at Grey Cloak, rose, and made his way over.

"Oh great, our nosy friend is back," Grey Cloak said.

"Perhaps he can help."

"No, keep quiet about it."

"Good evening, friends. I saw you helping out with the fire," Archi said. "I'd like to say thanks and buy you some hot cider."

"No, thank you," Anya said.

"Why the long faces?" Archi dragged a chair over and sat down. "You seem troubled. The trouble is over, and the fire is gone."

"True, and we are glad of it," Anya said, "and very tired.

If you would please excuse us, Archi, we'd like to enjoy the fire before we turn in."

He lifted his hands in surrender and said, "I understand. You're quarreling. Been there myself. I always found the best way to end the quarreling is to pucker up and kiss."

"No, we aren't together," Anya insisted. "If you please."

"Sure, sure." Archi started to rise, and when he did, he looked down at the hearth. "Say, where is that lizard of yours?" He lowered his voice. "I would say dragon, but that tends to catch the wrong ears sometimes."

Grey Cloak turned his head away from Archi.

"Aw... you lost him, did you? In the fire? Someone stole him?" Archi clawed at the curly hairs of his beard. "I hate to hear that. Those dragons are valuable. People will buy them, steal them, and fight them. I know this because I know it all. Seen all sorts, wandering through Loose Boot. It's a peaceful town, but it has an insidious underbelly too." His friendly tone darkened. "A misbegotten ilk that preys on strangers that are passing through."

32

Archi's words made Grey Cloak's neck hairs stand on end. He twisted around in his seat and looked Archibald West dead in the eye. "What are you getting at?"

"I'll tell you what I'm getting at, boy." Archi leaned over the table with his forearm sliding forward. "I want to know what that dragon is worth to you."

"Did you steal my dragon?" He started to rise from his seat.

"Sit down, boy, and keep your head on. I didn't say that I had your dragon, but I might know who does." Archi resumed his friendly voice and leaned back. "That dragon of yours is a runt, very, very valuable. The monarchs and the barons will fill up coffers full of coin for them. Coin that will keep me from breaking my back in the timberland for the rest of my life."

Anya sneered. "You are disgusting."

"No, I'm a businessman." His gaze landed on her. "And I take you for a Sky Rider."

She stiffened and drew her cloak tight around her.

"No sense hiding it from me. As I've said before, I've seen all sorts. I know a dragon rider when I see one. You wouldn't be the first to mosey through Loose Boot, and you won't be the last. At least you aren't a show-off like the others."

"What do you want?" Grey Cloak asked.

"I'm not a greedy man. Neither is my crew." He nodded at the group of rugged, fur-covered woodsmen sitting back at his table. "We are simple men, satisfied with a simple life, but we can get greedy from time to time."

"Will you spit it out?" Anya asked.

"Certainly. First off, open up that cloak," he said to Grey Cloak.

He did as the man requested. "I have a sword and dagger. A purse of coins."

"Hmm, put them aside, by the fire." Archi turned his attention to Anya. "You're a different story. I want that suit of armor and your sword belt. I know that its craft is priceless. That should set me and my men up for a good while."

"Are you really foolish enough to take on a Sky Rider?" Anya asked.

"The bigger the risk, the bigger the reward." Archi sucked his teeth and leered at her. "Besides, I don't think that you would want word to spread back to Dark Mountain that a Sky Rider is so near. This place would be covered in Riskers and their dragons. I think I'm offering you a very fair deal."

Grey Cloak and Anya's eyes met.

"You don't have to do this," he said.

"I do." She nodded at him and turned her eyes back on Archi. "Fine, my weapons and my armor in exchange for the dragon. Do we have a deal?"

"We have a deal. Come with me."

ARCHIBALD WEST AND HIS MEN, with a pack of timber wolves in tow, led Grey Cloak and Anya on a steep march into the mountains. The bearish thief bound their hands behind their backs and disarmed them of all of their weapons.

With snow blowing in his face, Archi said, "It's quite a climb. Quite a climb. Makes it difficult for escaping."

Grey Cloak twisted against the ropes that bound him. One thing was certain—they could tie an excellent knot. He might as well have had steel wrapped around his wrists.

Anya slipped down to a knee. The bearish brood of brigands helped her back to her feet.

"Don't touch me!" she said.

"She's a fiery one. I wouldn't expect anything less from

a Sky Rider!" Archi bellowed. "I bet you didn't think you'd come across a den of thieves like us up here. We're snow brigands. A different breed. We call ourselves the Wolf Pack."

"No matter what you call yourself, it's nothing to be proud of," Anya stated.

"Maybe not to you, but I'm proud of what I've caught," Archi replied.

They made it to the top of the hill, where the mouth of an old mine shaft awaited them. A pair of torches lit up the entrance, and two more brigands were standing guard outside, armed with spears.

"Inside," Archi ordered his men.

With firm shoves in the back, Grey Cloak and Anya were pushed through the entrance and led down a tunnel burrowed deep into the mountain. All of them had to stoop to walk.

"This used to be a gold mine, but that shining vein of gold was drained centuries ago. Now it fills the monarchs' treasure rooms and changes hands in the streets. Something like we are going to do."

"Thanks for the history lesson, but I couldn't care less," Grey Cloak said. "Take me to my dragon."

"We're almost there," Archi said. He let his timber wolf, Jock, squeeze by his knees and take the lead. "Let them know we're coming, Jock."

The passage opened up into a massive chamber. A

firepit was burning in the middle, the smoke rising into a hole that looked like a chimney. Torches lined the outer walls of the chamber, giving it warm illumination. Cots, furs, and blankets served as beds. There was a throne made of antlers and ram horns, and the pelts and heads of animals, from bears to mountain goats, lined the walls.

"For what it's worth, it's sort of cozy in here," Grey Cloak said under his breath to Anya.

"Don't get too cozy," she said.

Archi slung a heavy coat of fur off his shoulders, shook the snow off, and hung it on the back of his throne. He sat down in the chair and made himself comfortable.

The snow brigands brought Grey Cloak and Anya before Archi and made them kneel like he was some kind of king. Jock lay down at his feet and yawned.

They weren't alone in the room, either. Ten brigands had escorted them to the hideout, and ten more were waiting inside. They stood back against the wall, armed with swords and hatchets. Each and every one of them was wearing a large animal's pelt of some kind. Their timber wolves sat down by their feet.

Two of the brigands set a cage down in front of Archi. Streak was inside, balled up with his tail wrapped around his body.

Grey Cloak's heart sped up. He was thrilled his dragon was alive. He looked up at Archi, meeting the man's heavy stare, and got a sinking feeling in his stomach. "What are we waiting for, Archibald?"

Archi glowered at both of them and said, "I'm not waiting for anything. Everything I need is right here."

33

"Why the sudden change of heart?" Anya asked bitterly. "You agreed to take my armor and my weapons in a fair exchange for the dragon."

"Your armor and weapons have value, but they don't have the same value as you, Sky Rider," Archi said. A table with a goblet and a wine bowl was on the side of his throne. He dipped the goblet into the bowl and filled it, then he drank, letting the wine drip from the goblet and soak into his beard. "Today," he bellowed, "the Wolf Pack celebrates!"

The snow brigands howled like wolves, and their dogs joined him. The sound was deafening.

"Keep him talking, whatever you do," Grey Cloak said to Anya underneath the roar of the crowd. "Fight with him. Argue with him."

"Why?" she asked.

"I have an idea." They were outnumbered twenty to two, and that didn't include the wolves. It would be impossible for them to fight them if they didn't get any help. Grey Cloak could only think of one kind of help. He started concentrating on his cloak.

Archi lifted his big arm. "Silence." The howling was cut short. He leaned forward and said, "Now that we have gotten to know one another, I'd like to know what your name is."

"Why is that?" Anya asked.

"That information will be very important to the Riskers when I send a message to them. A name can carry great weight. Why else would they come?"

"I'll tell you nothing."

Archi tilted his head at one of his men. "I imagine that you are a stubborn one. Perhaps a taste from my fire will loosen your tongue."

"I doubt it. Don't you know that Sky Riders are resistant to fire?"

"We'll see about that." One of Archi's men pulled a poker free from the flames.

Using thought, Grey Cloak managed to get his inner pocket to push out the Figurine of Heroes. It fell to the ground in front of his knees. He tried to hide it by shifting forward.

But Archi caught the move. He stabbed his finger at the figurine. "What is that? Bring it to me!"

A brigand in snow leopard skin hurried over and picked up the figurine. He gave it to Archi and moved back to his post.

"What is this?" Archi asked as he rubbed his fingers over the polished figurine.

"I like to carve," Grey Cloak said. "I was making a figurine of you and your bloated head. As you can see, it's not finished yet. I think I'm going to need material to get the head right. Ha. It could be a figurine of its own."

"Do you take me for a fool? I know wizardry when I see it," Archi said. "Gag him."

"Why? Did I say something offensive?" Grey Cloak began summoning the words in his mind, and his lips started to tingle. It had been so long that he wasn't sure that he could recall them.

"Leave him be," Anya said loudly, "and I'll tell you my name and his, you fool!"

"You'll tell me now! What is it?"

"Priscilla Pickle!"

"That's it! Burn her cheek!" Archi commanded. He set the figurine down on his table. "That will get it out of her!"

The back-and-forth argument went on. The words started to flow from Grey Cloak's tongue as the brigands got caught up in the argument. He closed his eyes and finished the mystic words that unleashed the figurine's dark secret.

The Figurine of Heroes fell over and rolled off the table. It didn't stop rolling until it stood up between Archibald's throne and Grey Cloak. Inky-black smoke started to spit out of the figurine's head.

The brigand leader's shifty eyes grew like saucers. He pulled his weapon, and so did his men. "What devilry is this, trickster?"

"I don't have the slightest idea what is going on."

The timber wolves began to howl, and a figure began to take form in the smoke. As the smoke began to clear, it revealed a lean, bald man dressed in crimson-and-black wizard's robes. His black eyebrows had a sharp peak in them, and he had the air of the cunning of a wolf. A jug of wine was in his hand, and he had gaudy rings on many of his fingers. The man eyed Archi and asked, "What do you want, fat one?"

Archi swallowed as he stood with sword in hand. "I am Archibald West, leader of the Wolf Pack. Who, might I ask, are you?"

"I am the Keeper of Secrets, Blacksmith of the Mystic Forge, the Jaded Servant, the Gray Fox, the Inept Caster, the Insane Slayer, king maker, wine drinker, Black Spell, Scarab Bearer, Friend of the Blue-Toe, but most importantly, I am Finster, Master of the Inanimate." With the hawkish eyes of a predator, he scanned the room. He took a drink from his jug. "I'll ask one more time. Why have you summoned me?"

Grey Cloak spoke up. "He didn't summon you. I did."

Finster glowered down at him and said, "Well, that was a mistake."

34

G rey Cloak's mind started to race. He'd heard that using the Figurine of Heroes could be a gamble, but he hadn't expected it to turn on him so soon. He tried to summon his wizardry and burn his bonds away. *This isn't working. That man is insane.*

"Ew, it smells like dog in here." Finster finished off his jug and tossed it aside. "You wouldn't have anything to drink, would you? Preferably wine? Lots of it."

The wary-eyed Archibald offered a crooked smile. "Anything you like, wizard."

"Grey Cloak, what have you done?" Anya asked as she strained against her bonds.

"What is this?" Finster cast his gaze at Anya and smiled. "Well, well, well, a damsel in distress. It appears that I've misjudged the situation. It's known to happen when you are inebriated." He swayed from side to side. "Where am I, anyway? A kennel?"

Grey Cloak's fingers started to spark, and his leather cords began to burn. He kept talking. "Finster, I summoned you to help us." He looked at Archibald. "They took us against our will."

"Let me get this straight," Finster said, slurring a bit when he spoke, and tapped his fingers on the side of his head. He pointed at Grey Cloak. "You summoned me to rescue you and her"—he winked at Anya and pointed at Archi—"from him?"

"Yes!" Grey Cloak and Anya said together.

Finster nodded. "That makes more sense." He interlocked his fingers and cracked his knuckles.

"Wizard, you are making a grave mistake," Archi threatened. "Our numbers are superior. My men are skilled. We will slaughter you. All of you."

"That's hardly the plea for mercy that I was expecting," Finster said as he cracked his neck from side to side. "Let's get on with it, shall we?"

Archibald West thrust his sword upward and bellowed, "Wolf Pack, kill him!"

Finster passed his gaudily clad fingers in front of his eyes. "I don't think so."

In the wink of an eye, the sharp weapon of every brigand, including Archibald, was ripped from their fingers and hovered before them, pointing at their chests. The men froze in their tracks, eyeing their weapons and gaping.

"Now you know why they call me the Master of the Inanimate." Finster waved his hand. The suspended weapons waved with him. He pushed his hand forward, and the weapons backed the brigands against the wall.

Archibald dropped back in his chair, his own sword touching his chest. His eyes were filled with horror.

"Milady," Finster said politely to Anya, "you might want to look away for this. The execution can be quite gruesome."

Grey Cloak felt his heart beating in his throat as Finster thrust his arm forward. Every sword plunged through the brigands' furs and into their chests. Anya gasped. Grey Cloak's blood went cold, but the cords that bound him gave way to his extinguishing fire. The timber wolves bayed as their brigand masters slid down the walls and fell dead.

"Oh, shut up!" Finster said.

With their ears lowered, the pack of wolves scurried out of the brigands' den and vanished into the corridor. Archibald lay dead in his throne with his eyes still open.

Finster helped himself to the man's bowl of wine. "Ah, I always get thirsty after a hard day's work. What is the name of this place?"

"Gapoli," Grey Cloak said as he fetched a dagger, then he cut away Anya's bonds.

She was pale when she said, "I've never seen an execution like that."

"I am very efficient, young lady." Finster nodded at her as his body started to fade into smoke. "A pleasure meeting the both of you. Especially you, Red. Can I have your na—"

The inky smoke made a cone funnel that sank back into the shape of the figurine.

"That was the most horrifying thing I've ever seen," Anya said, her face glistening with sweat. "Does that Finster always come?"

"No." Grey Cloak picked up the figurine, stuck it in his cloak pocket, and freed Streak from his cage. The dragon climbed into his hood. "It's always someone different."

"I thought he was going to kill us."

"It wouldn't have been the first time that happened, based on what I've been told."

Anya found her sword belt and buckled it on. "I can live with your decision, seeing how Archi was planning to kill us in the end. But I don't think I'd trust you using that object again." She eyed the dead. "I've seen my share of battles, but that was cold and gruesome."

"It's better than being on the inside of a grave," he replied.

More brigands rushed into the room, but once they saw their dead brethren, they turned around and ran.

"That was easy. Shall we go?" Grey Cloak asked.

Together, they hustled through the passage and back

outside, into the wintry night. The brigands had abandoned their posts, and fresh tracks from both men and wolves were on the freshly fallen snow. With the wind in their faces, Grey Cloak and Anya made their way to the bottom of the slippery slope. At the bottom, a man was sitting in a single-horse-drawn wagon, waiting. He was covered up in a wool blanket.

"Need a ride?" the man asked in a friendly voice.

They approached with caution.

"Who are you?" Grey Cloak asked.

The man uncovered his head. He was older, paunchy, with a head of thick brown hair. A warm smile covered his face. "I'm Crane. Tanlin sent me to fetch you."

"Tanlin? Really?"

"Why else would I be out here on a night like this?" Crane replied. "Come on, hop in. I'm freezing to death."

"You don't have to ask me twice." Anya took a seat beside Crane.

Grey Cloak climbed in the back.

Crane whipped his lash and said, "Onward, Vixen. Onward."

35

Grey Cloak, Anya, and Crane made camp in the lower hills of the mountains where Cinder was sleeping. The grand dragon was buried in a foot of snow already. No one would know that a dragon was lying underneath.

"I'm so happy that he is alive," Grey Cloak said as he rubbed his hands over the campfire. He'd been grinning from ear to ear ever since Crane told him that Dyphestive was alive and well. "Tell me more."

Crane was wearing wool mitts and drinking from a metal cup of coffee. "Talon is waiting for the Doom Riders to exit Dark Mountain. Thanks to Zora, Dyphestive will be ready when the moment comes to make a hasty escape. Of course, that is easier said than done, given that they have Doom Riders to contend with."

"How is Zora doing?" Grey Cloak asked.

"Quite well, and I've grown very fond of her in the short time that we've spent together. She was very brave to go into the mountain to look for your friend. Most spies that go in never come out again." Craned winced when he took a sip. "Horsefeathers, that's hot." He lifted his gaze to Anya. "Would you like a cup?"

"No, I'm fine, thank you," she said with frosty breath.

"At least get a blanket or something. I have extra in my wagon." Crane winced again. "Just looking at you in that cloak and metal armor makes *me* freeze to death."

Grey Cloak was warm in his cloak. He hadn't given it much thought, but he hadn't been cold at all in the north. He recalled what Batram had said about the Cloak of Legends having many wonders. "Would you like my cloak, Anya?" he offered.

"No, you can keep that creepy thing." She sat down on a hunk of dead wood that they'd rolled up alongside the fire. Her pretty eyes caught Grey Cloak's. "I'm glad to hear that they found Dyphestive. He is very sweet, and I wish you well rescuing him."

"You aren't coming?" he asked.

"Of course not, even though I wish I could. I've grown fond of our adventures." Her green eyes reflected the flickering flames of the fire. "But I have to return to Gunder Island and face the Sky Riders. My actions will have consequences, and I will be held responsible for them. Besides, I have a sleeping dragon to tend to. There's no telling how long until he wakes up again. Hopefully no more than a week or two."

"*A week or two?*" Crane asked. "You can't wait out here that long. You'll freeze to death."

"I assure you that I'll be fine. Sky Riders know how to survive when they are grounded."

"At least go back to Loose Boot and stay warm," Grey Cloak argued.

"After what we just ran into? No, I think I'll take my chances in the mountains. Besides, I like the peace and quiet. I need time to think." She pulled her cloak tight over her shoulders and smirked. "That was a nice trick you pulled in the Wolf Pack's lair."

Crane arched an eyebrow.

Grey Cloak replied, "Which trick?"

"Burning through your cords using wizardry. I hadn't even thought about that."

He stretched out his hands. "Well, there's a price for it." His wrists had raw red marks on them. "All I can say is be careful. I should have been able to loosen the rope myself, but those snow brigands really knew what they were doing. I'm pretty sure we weren't their first hostages."

"No, but I believe we are the last." She giggled.

"What happened up on that hill?" Crane asked.

"You don't want to know," she said, "and I'd rather not

think about it. How did you find us? That's what I want to know."

"I rolled into Loose Boot, and within an hour, I had learned that you'd been taken away by the Wolf Pack." Crane warmed up his coffee cup from the kettle that sat on the fire. "The Brotherhood of Whispers has an eye and an ear out for everything. We always know what is going on. So I followed their trail up into the hills and waited. I have to tell you, I'm glad that you made it out. I wasn't looking forward to figuring out how to get you out. That's not my specialty."

"What *is* your specialty?" Grey Cloak asked.

"Knowing things and keeping my neck out of trouble. A man like me does draw suspicion, even though, well, I am pretty handsome."

"So now what?" Grey Cloak asked. "We wait until morning and head back to Dark Mountain to find Dyphestive?" He gave Anya a guilty glance. "The truth is, I'm ready to go now."

"I'll be fine. I think you know me well enough to know that I can take care of myself. Not to mention that I have Cinder." She reached over and put her hand on his arm. "Dyphestive needs you. Go and get him."

His throat tightened. "I will. I can't—"

"Say no more, Grey Cloak. We'll meet again. I'm sure of it."

By horse and wagon, Grey Cloak and Crane rode off into the night without saying so much as a word. Grey Cloak couldn't wash away an image of Anya standing in the snow, all alone. His heart ached.

Finally, Crane broke the silence and said, "You're awfully quiet. Care to share what is on your mind? It's going to be a long, long ride."

"She risked an awful lot for me. I feel... guilty."

"Don't feel guilty. She gave you a gift. Accept it. Besides, she's a good woman. In her heart, she did right. She knows that, or she wouldn't have done it."

Grey Cloak frowned. "Yes, but you don't know the Sky Riders. They'll punish her because of me."

"Perhaps. Perhaps not." Crane leaned over and nudged his shoulder. "You're fond of her, aren't you?"

"Well, yes."

"No, I mean really fond of her." Crane waggled his eyebrows.

"Not like that. She's old."

"Ha! She's a beautiful woman, and I sensed a connection between the two of you. When she touched your arm, I could have sworn I saw a spark."

"You're mad." He turned away, and his cheeks felt flushed. *Am I blushing? Why am I blushing? I don't like her. Not like that.*

"Do you know what I think?" Crane asked.

"I don't want to know. Please, stop talking."

"Care if I sing?"

"Go ahead."

36

Crane's wagon rumbled down the road toward Kenna, a small community in the northern plains of Westerlund. The wagon rocked from side to side, as the horse, Vixen, pulled them out of a rut.

"Come on, girl. Haul us out!" Crane said with a flick of his lash. The wagon heaved up and down with jarring impact. "Whoa, that was a rough patch. But it's better than those mountains. A man can freeze his nanoos off if he spends too much time there."

"Can't we go any faster?" Grey Cloak asked. His arms were crossed, and he pitched gently from side to side. "Vixen can go faster, can't she?"

"We've trotted some. And Vixen isn't a spring chicken. She is getting old, and I don't want her to lose a shoe."

"You have a box of shoes and tools in the back."

Crane gave an incredulous look, as he often did when he was speaking. "I still don't want her to lose one. They are lucky."

"Of course." He rolled his eyes. "If I ran, it would be much faster."

"True, but how would you know where you were going?"

"The question is, how do *you* know where we are going?"

"Ah!" Crane raised a stubby finger. "I've been waiting for you to ask that. I know where we are going because I have this." He produced a brass box that filled his hand and was shaped like a beetle. The beetle wings had runes all over them. "Watch this."

Crane twisted the wings off like a cap. "To the naked eye, it looks like a maiden's jewelry box, but what is inside is a surprise."

The body of the beetle was filled with black grains of sand that twinkled in the light. Along the top rim of the circle was a tiny emerald stone. Crane slowly spun the beetle around in a full circle, but the emerald didn't move. It slid inside the sand and remained in place.

"What is it?" Grey Cloak asked.

Crane poked his finger at the green dot and said excitedly, "That emerald is Tanlin. As long as we follow the emerald, we find him. He has the medallion of location. I gave it to him." He nudged Grey Cloak. "The

Brotherhood of Secrets. Always prepared. Always secret."

"If the emerald is on the rim, that means they are still far away?"

"That's right. Once it moves inside the rim, we know they are within fifty leagues. The emerald will stop in the middle when we are right on top of them. Fascinating, isn't it?"

"Absolutely, but can it help pick up this agonizing pace?"

To Grey Cloak's chagrin, Crane insisted that they stop in Kenna and stay the night. "Vixen needs her rest. She's no good to us if she's tired," he'd said.

They shared a meal in a local tavern that was rich in stream salmon and tasty spirits. Crane enjoyed singing with the locals onstage and showed he was a master of the stringed instrument. He even smoked a cigar when he played.

Sitting at the table, Grey Cloak fed chunks of fish and bread into his hood for Streak to gobble up. He wasn't going to take any more chances by letting his runt dragon run free. That had gotten them into plenty of trouble the last time.

"Come on, get up here and sing!" Crane shouted at him.

Grey Cloak waved Crane off. The man was a little too jolly for his liking. For the time being, he preferred to lie low and sulk in the corner with his back to the wall. A small green vase with a white daisy was in the center of the table. He pulled the flower free and turned it in his fingers. As eager as he was to reunite with Dyphestive, he couldn't stop thinking about Anya. Her big green eyes and wavy red hair were stuck in his mind.

He started plucking the petals. *She likes me. She doesn't like me. She likes me. She doesn't like me. She likes me.*

Streak's tail flicked out of the hood and smacked Grey Cloak across the eyes.

"Are you still hungry?" He stabbed the rest of the salmon with his fork and fed it back into his hood. "Eat!"

A barmaid gave him a funny look as she walked by.

"Do you mind? Sometimes I need a treat in the middle of the night. And I paid for it!"

The waitress hurried away.

"Goodness, am I that cranky?" He set the flower aside.

I don't miss her. I don't miss her. I don't miss her. He squeezed his eyes shut and blanked all images of Anya out. *Ah, that's better.*

Crane's jacket was hanging on the back of the chair. The red-faced Crane was singing at the top of his lungs and working the patrons into the sing-along. Grey Cloak reached inside Crane's coat pocket and pulled out the bronze beetle box. Keeping the box low in his lap, he twisted the lid off.

The tiny emerald gem had moved away from the rim and toward the middle. He nearly jumped from his seat. For the longest time, he moved the box around and watched it intently. Ever so slowly, the gemstone pushed its way through the sand. He almost didn't believe his eyes, but he was certain of it.

"Talon is coming," he muttered, his whole body tingling. "Talon is near."

37

At the crack of dawn, Grey Cloak and Crane took off northeast.

A bleary-eyed Crane handled the reins and asked, "Did we have to leave so early?" He opened his mouth in a wide yawn. "I'm not an early riser. I'm more of a midmorning man. I like to snuggle my head in my feather pillow and wake up gradually."

"If you hadn't stayed up all night singing, it wouldn't be a problem," Grey Cloak said. He was holding the bronze locator box, his eyes glued on the emerald. It had moved toward them, but now it moved away. "We need to go northeast."

"Toward Daggerford?"

"Yes."

"Will you quit staring at that thing?" Crane slapped at his hands. "You're going to burn your eyes out."

"I'm not going to burn my eyes out."

"You will if you keep using it wrong!" Crane reached for it. "Give it to me!"

Grey Cloak slid to the end of the bench and said, "I'm not using it wrong. And why are you so testy?"

"Why am I so testy? I'll tell you why!" Crane said with a snarl on his face and fire in his eyes. "Because you dragged me out of bed, and I haven't had my coffee!" He flicked his whip. "And you are using it wrong. You can't watch it like an hourglass. It will make you mad. Close it and check it again in a few hours. A wise man won't get lost if he follows directions."

"You're full of wisdom, aren't you?"

"Of course. I'm old, and you don't get to be this old by being stupid."

Grey Cloak twisted the lid back onto the location box and dropped it into one of his inner pockets. "I'll hang on to it, if you don't mind."

"Fine by me."

Streak popped his head out of Grey Cloak's hood, his tongue flicking out of his mouth, then he climbed out of the hood and took his place between them.

"Well, who do we have here?" Crane said cheerfully. "A hairless dog. I've never seen one so ugly before."

"Ha-ha," Grey Cloak said drily. "I'd watch what you say. He might bite your finger off."

"Aw, I was only teasing. He's a handsome little fella, like you." Crane stretched out his palm. "May I pet him?"

"That's up to him, not me."

The dragon's smoke-colored eyes were fixed on the road ahead. He sat like a dog, as stiff as a board.

Grey Cloak patted the dragon's head. "Be nice to the old man."

Crane started petting Streak like a cat. "I've seen many things, but I don't have much experience with dragons. You are a blessed man to have such a wondrous creature in your possession."

"It was either him or a really big one. They would have been hard to travel with, and I'm pretty sure one wouldn't have fit in my hood."

"Interesting, but isn't the entire point of being a Sky Rider being able to 'Ride the Sky'?" Crane stuck his palm out in a smooth motion when he said it.

"That's what they wanted, but I didn't feel ready. And I don't think those dragons were ready for me, either." He patted Streak on the head. "Besides, he was the only one that accepted me. The others hissed or curled away. I'm fine with it. But Streak and I need to bond more. We just haven't had much time for it."

"How much bigger will he get?"

"Not much. Hopefully my hood will still hold him."

Crane continued to stroke Streak's back. "I would do anything to fly on a dragon. It's a shame that we couldn't stick with Anya. I hoped that she might take me up in the sky." He gazed above. "Imagine soaring through the air like the birds that take it for granted. I'd do anything to spend my time in the heavens."

"Not if it makes you queasy."

"Oh?"

"Barrel-rolling through the sky isn't as exciting as you'd think. It made me as sick as a hound." He made a squeamish face. "One moment, your stomach is up in your mouth, and in the next moment, it's down in your toes."

Crane made a face too. "Well, don't ruin my fantasy."

"Sorry, I only thought that you should know what to expect in case it happens. Make sure that you don't eat a big lunch before you go, or you'll certainly lose it."

"You're strange for an elf."

"I like to think of myself as unique."

"That too."

They rode hour after hour, heading northeast toward Daggerford. It nearly killed Grey Cloak to not look at the locator box. Finally, Crane gave him the nod, and he twisted the cap off. The green gem had crept farther south and was still on track to meet with their location. "They are still coming our way."

"See? Everything is working out according to plan. You only need to be patient."

"I've been patient enough. It's been almost a year since I've seen my friends. Even worse, Dyphestive has been in Dark Mountain for a year. *A year.* I know how that place tries to control the minds of its people. And Dyphestive, well, he'd be lost without me. He's very naïve."

"Zora said that he was doing fine."

"Well, that certainly gives me hope. I hate the thought of him being on his own. And the mere thought of him being a Doom Rider. That is madness."

"The young are very strong-willed. I'm sure he's getting along fine, especially if he is set in his ways. Hopefully, he won't be susceptible to change. His heart is strong. His true nature will stay the same."

Grey Cloak recalled the awful night he'd encountered the Doom Riders and their horrible beasts. The evil brood was merciless. He hated to imagine that Dyphestive would become one of them, and he was determined more now than ever to save his friend. "Can't you speed this old mare up? We need to go faster."

38

DAGGERFORD

Talon followed the Doom Riders all the way to Daggerford. In the woodland less than a league away from town, they set up camp. The sun was setting on what had turned out to be a brisk evening, and Bowbreaker was reporting back.

"They settled in at a small tavern. Their gourn are stabled," he said. "All of Daggerford's whisperers are restless."

"I can imagine," Rhonna said. She was warming up beans and rice over the fire. "No one wants to host that sort of company."

Lythlenion, Tanlin, and Zora joined Rhonna by the fire. The older halfling, Cotton, was there, but he kept to himself and remained quiet.

Zora spoke up. "If you like, I can go and make contact with him. He's expecting me."

Rhonna took a burning stick out of the fire and lit the end of her cigar. "I'm thinking that might not be the best idea. You said you've talked with Drysis, and if she catches a glimpse of you, well, she might kill you."

"And I don't want to remind everyone that we almost died at the hands of the Scourge the last time we were here," Tanlin added. "It's very possible that our faces could be recognized."

"Daggerford's not that small," Zora said.

Tanlin pushed up his sleeves and stirred the pot. "It's small enough. The only one of us that hasn't been seen in Daggerford is Bowbreaker."

"I'm not going into that town. It's not my way," Bowbreaker said.

"You're the only one that can go," Rhonna argued.

Bowbreaker held an arrow and twirled it through his fingers. "I don't go anywhere without my bow."

"I don't think you carrying a bow into town is going to arouse any suspicion," Zora said. "But I'd be glad to accompany you."

"No, you've done enough." Rhonna blew out a stream of smoke. "Tanlin, what about that scarf of yours? Wouldn't that make it easier?"

Tanlin rubbed his scarf. "It would, but I can't stay invisible forever. I suppose it is the safest bet."

"You look pale," Rhonna said.

"That's because I can still feel the flames that almost burned us to death in that town. And I see visions of those Doom Riders slaying our friends. Pardon me for being a coward or feeling old, but I can't help it."

"You could let me use it," Zora suggested. "Besides, Dyphestive will be expecting me."

"Now you are going to shame me." Tanlin shook his head and wrapped his scarf around his neck. "No, I'll do it. Besides, I don't think Dyphestive is only expecting you. He should be expecting any of us."

"We'll be close," Rhonna said.

"What, you expect me to go *now*?" Tanlin asked.

"Yes, it's a busier time of the day. There'll be more distractions. And we don't expect you to kiss Dyphestive. Go in and see and listen," Rhonna said.

"I've done this before. Thanks for the lesson." Tanlin stood and said, "When you say near, how near?"

"Bowbreaker, since you're too chicken to head into town, you can wait at the camp with your kitty." Rhonna's eyes swept over the area. "Say, where is that sand cat?"

"Free," Bowbreaker said. "I can handle watching a fire."

Zora brightened and said, "And I'll stay here and help him."

Tanlin's tone didn't hide his disappointment. "Thanks for the support."

Rhonna shoved him in the back. "You'll be fine. You've got me and Lyth. Now march."

Cotton ambled after them. "May I go?"

Though Rhonna gave him a doubtful look, she said, "Sure, come along."

BOW IN HAND, Bowbreaker stood tall, facing Daggerford, which lay to the south. His silence made him all the more imposing as the evening winds stirred his jet-black hair.

Zora scooped beans and rice into a bowl, her heart beating like a jackhammer. It was the first time she'd been alone with the elf that she found so attractive. She took a quick breath and walked it over to him. *Don't make a fool of yourself. Settle down. He's just another elf.*

"I made you a bowl of beans," she said politely.

"Why?" he asked in his stern manner, not even giving her a glance. "I didn't ask for any."

"I thought you might be hungry."

"Do I look hungry?"

"Uh, no," she said.

"Then why would you think that?"

Zora's mouth made an O. She turned her back, shuffled away, and squatted by the fire again. "Fine. I'll eat it." She started to burn inside. "And forgive me for trying to be kind to the king of conversation."

Bowbreaker turned his head. "Why would you call me the king of conversation? I don't speak so much."

"No, but you just set a new mark for yourself." Zora dug her spoon into the bowl and started eating in silence. She could feel Bowbreaker's heavy stare on her, so she turned her shoulders away.

After a long pause, Bowbreaker finally said, "Ah, you made a jest about me, didn't you?"

She shrugged.

Bowbreaker took a seat beside her and laid his bow behind him. "Have I offended you, Zora?"

"I was trying to get to know you better. After all, we are all out here risking our lives for one another." She set down the bowl with a frown. "I don't know what is worse—the beans and rice or the conversation."

Bowbreaker tossed his head back and let out a hearty laugh. "Ha-ha-ha! Ah-ha-ha-ha!"

She gave him a bewildered look. "What are you laughing at?"

"I found your statement very amusing." His stony demeanor warmed. "I will set some snares, and you can feast on the varmints. Many of their juices are succulent when properly prepared."

The corners of her mouth turned up in a smile. "I would like that."

39

Tanlin left Rhonna and Lythlenion on the edge of town and wandered into the streets of Daggerford. The hardy citizens were abuzz with news of the arrival of the Doom Riders. A host of people was gathered outside of the White Salt tavern, on the eastern edge of town, hiding behind porch posts and lingering on the decks above. Their eyes were fixed on the single-story red-roofed tavern that the notorious riders had entered.

"This should be interesting," Tanlin muttered as he moseyed down the streets, blending in with the onlookers he passed. He hadn't used the Scarf of Shadows yet, but his fingers clung to the fabric.

Standing on a porch across the street, he craned his neck and asked a pudgy woman in a brick-red dress, "What is going on?"

"Doom Riders," she said with excitement. "Can you believe it? They say that whenever a Doom Rider comes, people die."

"And you're standing around here?"

Her eyes were fixed on the tavern door. "Of course. I want to see what happens."

"You mean you want to see someone die," he said.

"We don't get much excitement around here. It's a sleepy town, and we keep to ourselves. But I've been here all my life, never seen a Doom Rider. Not going to miss it, either." She twisted her head around and blinked. "Say, where'd you go?"

Tanlin had moved down the porch and was watching the front door. A man hurried out of the tavern with his fist holding his pants up. His suspenders were broken, and his face was ashen. He tripped and fell in the dust.

A huge man with flame-red hair swung out of the tavern's entrance. He had a jug of wine in one hand and a sword in the other.

A cold sensation swept through Tanlin's limbs. There was no mistaking the man in dragon-scale-leather armor. It was a Doom Rider but without the mask. It didn't make the man any more human.

"Where are you going?" the Doom Rider asked. He drank from his jug, slammed it on the porch, and marched down the street. "We aren't finished playing our game yet."

Daggerford's citizens hunkered down in their hiding

spots. They all froze like deer that have heard a sound in the woods.

Tanlin's own head sank into his shoulders, and he kept his eyes down. He could still see the Doom Riders slaying the overmatched Adanadel and Browning like they were nothing, and they'd been seasoned fighters.

The disheveled man in the street crab-walked away from the Doom Rider. "I'm sorry. I'm sorry. Please don't kill me. You won all my chips. I have nothing left."

"I know that. But I didn't say that you could leave." The square-jawed Doom Rider picked the man up by the collar and lifted him to his toes. The man's pants fell down.

No one laughed. No one even breathed.

The Doom Rider dragged the pleading man down the street and hauled him back into the tavern. The huge man stopped inside the doorway and hollered, "Any of you cowards wanting to play? Come on in! But no one leaves until I say you leave!" He shut himself back inside.

The local folk breathed sighs of relief in unison and began muttering.

One man in blue trousers and a knit hat said, "I'd do it, but I don't have any chips."

Another with a pipe in his mouth replied, "Let me hold your hat."

The man in blue trousers complied.

"You don't need chips, just some steel in your back." He shoved the man in blue trousers into the street.

Horror filled the man's eyes, as if he were standing in quicksand. He leapt as if for his very life back onto the porch.

Some of the locals burst out laughing.

"Don't you do that again, Earl!" the man in blue trousers said. He snatched back his knit hat and stuffed it on his head. "I'm going home!"

These people are demented, Tanlin thought.

He moved on, heading farther down the road, where he could cross the street without notice. Waiting for the sun to set, he made his way along the rear of the buildings that faced east. He'd considered going into a tavern without invisibility. Chances were that the Doom Riders might not know his face, and he did a fine job blending in. But the plan had to be scrapped the moment he realized that the Doom Riders were making a spectacle of everything.

He pulled the Scarf of Shadows over his nose and watched his hand vanish. Even though he'd grown used to it, not seeing himself was an unsettling feeling that stirred his stomach every time he did it. *Here I go. May the Lords of the Air be with me.*

The tavern had a back door and open windows. He peeked through one of the windows and saw a skeleton crew of two men in greasy aprons working up a sweat in the kitchen. They grumbled to one another and kept their heads down.

Tanlin climbed through the window and down onto the

floor. Even though he was invisible, it was his natural inclination to move out of sight or in the shadows. The scarf's powers were unpredictable from time to time, but as long as he wasn't manhandled or jostled firmly, he would remain hidden.

A swinging door led out into the tavern's main floor. He made his approach, but the door blasted open, missing him by a nose. His heart jumped, and he froze in place. The man who'd opened it was only inches from touching him.

A Doom Rider with nasty red scars all over his face was standing at the threshold. "If either of you goes anywhere, you're dead!" he said. "Now get our dinner ready. I'm hungry." He moved back into the tavern.

And put some mint leaves on his plate. His breath is awful. As the door swung open again, Tanlin slipped through and let out an almost audible gasp.

40

___

Drysis the Dreadful was standing in front of the bar, facing Tanlin. There was no mistaking the white braids of her shoulder-length hair or her eye patch. She was tall for a woman, too, as tall as her men, if not taller. She was leaning over, sipping wine from one of the five goblets. Her good eye, the right one, was locked on him.

She sees me. She sees me. He was standing in the kitchen doorway, so he had to move before someone moved into him.

The man with scars took his place beside Drysis and asked, "Are you going to drink or sip?"

Drysis broke her stare and said, "Sip." With her goblet in hand, she turned her back to the bar.

Phew! Tanlin wiped the sweat from his brow. He'd barely made it inside the tavern and felt like he'd had two brushes with death. He wasn't the sort of man to put up much of a fight. If they caught him, they would kill him and possibly torture him first.

With the air rife with tension, he stole his way past the bar and moved deeper into the tavern. The Doom Riders weren't alone. It appeared as if the tavern dwellers had been taken hostage the moment the Doom Riders appeared. The patrons were sitting at their round table, as stiff as dead squirrels, with their eyes down on their cold food.

As Tanlin made his way to a nook by the fire, he made an account of all the riders according to what Dyphestive had told Zora about them. Ghost still had his dyed-blue leather skull mask on, and he was standing at the front door, as still as a statue.

The bare-faced man with red hair, Shamrok, was the only one making any sort of ruckus. He was sitting at a table, playing cards with three locals and Dyphestive.

Dyphestive was still wearing his black skull mask, and his dragon-scale armor was well fitted. His broad girth made him appear huge. The four cards he was holding were small in his tremendous hands.

Scar moved away from the long bar to a small stage on the other side of the room. A man in brown trousers and suspenders was laid out cold on the stage. Another man, an orc, trembled as he held a fiddle.

"Play something I like this time. Something that will make these folks pick their feet up and dance."

The orc fiddler nodded, his chin trembling, and drew his bow across the strings, making it give an upbeat whine.

Scar began clapping and stomping. "That's more like it." He grabbed a young barmaid by the arm and jerked her up from her chair then clutched her tight to his chest. "You'll dance with me, little flower, and like it." He gave her a big kiss on the cheek. "I ain't so bad."

Tanlin's chest tightened. Daggerford wasn't the most innocent place. It took in all sorts that wanted to live in peace and with discretion. Their quiet existence had been invaded, and they would have to weather the storm and hope it didn't last long. But it wasn't them that Tanlin was worried about. It was Dyphestive.

"Play your hand, Iron Bones," Shamrok said as he dropped a few silver chips on the table. "The same as the rest of you."

Everyone added chips to the pile. Two of the locals that were playing were shaking.

Shamrok dropped his four cards on the table and gave a crooked grin. "Three red sparrows. Beat that." He looked at Dyphestive's cards. "You lose." He addressed the next man and the next. "You lose. You lose." Lifting an eyebrow, he said, "Well, what do we have here?" He eyeballed the pale-faced card player's cards. "I see four crows. Four crows! That beats my three sparrows! Is that right?"

"Y-yes, I suppose it does." Sweat dripped down the pale-faced man's cheek. He swallowed. "I'm sorry."

"No, by all means, take your prize," Shamrok said politely. "You won it fairly." He reached over and rubbed the man's small shoulders. "Looks like you are really good at playing Birds. Aren't you?"

The man nodded and said with a shaky voice, "I've been known to gamble." He reached for the coins.

Shamrok's grip tightened on the man's shoulder, and the man grimaced and shrank back.

"I'm a gambler too." Shamrok's voice became low and dangerous. "And I know that the odds of drawing four crows in one hand is highly unlikely. As I understand it, it's nearly impossible. Methinks you are a cheater. Are you a cheater?"

The man didn't want to nod. Tanlin could tell because of the way the man eyed the pile of chips like it was his. But the man caved in and nodded.

"Ha! That means I win." With one large paw, Shamrok raked the coins toward him. "As for you, cheater, well, I don't play with men that don't play honestly. I kill them." He pulled a dagger.

The crowd gasped.

Shamrok punched the man in the face with the pommel, and the man fell backward out of his chair, out cold. Shamrok put his dagger away. "Ha, only jesting." He eyed the other two men. "This time."

A cook in the back stuck his head out of the door and said, "Your dinner is ready to serve."

Scar set down the barmaid he'd danced with, turned toward the cook, and replied, "What are you waiting for? Put it on the table." He strolled across the tavern and pulled out a chair for Drysis.

She sat down and set her rotating crossbow on the table. It was the very same one that she'd killed Dalsay with, loaded with four bolts that were ready to go.

Tanlin couldn't fight the chills running through him as the cook and the barmaids set the meal on the table. He watched Scar and Drysis eat and talk quietly while the other patrons eyed them with horror. Narrowing his eyes and perking his ears, Tanlin began to sort out what they were saying. *Ah, they are meeting somebody? Who might that be?* He read Drysis's lips. *Oh no. The Scourge is coming!*

41

Tanlin sorted through his thoughts, trying to decide whether or not to warn the others now or hang around and gather more information. The situation was bad enough with the Doom Riders, but Talon's archrival was being added to the mix. *And here we are severely outnumbered and overmatched. This is awful.*

His gaze hung on Dyphestive. He didn't come to save the youth, but he at least wanted to try to get him a message. But something about the young man had changed. Dyphestive, easygoing and generally cheerful, was sitting upright and moving little. It was as if his mind was not his own. *Something really is off about him.*

"Take that mask off," Shamrok said as he reached over and pulled off Dyphestive's mask. "Show these folks what a handsome fella you are, like me." He grinned and slapped the deck of cards in front of him. "Now deal."

Dyphestive's messy blond hair was damp with sweat. His face was expressionless, cold, like Drysis's. He had a lost look in his eyes. One by one, he started dealing the cards to the others at the table.

Tanlin's heart ached for the young man. The boyish face he'd once known had been replaced with hard lines. As much as he hated to admit it, it looked like the Dyphestive he'd known was gone, replaced by a man that had killed a group of halflings. But he wanted to be sure. *If I could get him away from the others, perhaps I could whisper in his ear and see what he recognizes. How in the world will I do that?*

He let out a silent sigh. *There's nothing more that I can do here. I'd better go.*

On cat's feet, he crept back through the tavern toward the bar. He was halfway across the room when a rotted floorboard groaned loudly beneath his foot.

One woman jumped in her chair.

A man asked, "What is that?"

Ghost pushed his back off the wall and stared toward the sound.

Drysis's gaze locked on Tanlin's location too. "Did you hear that?" she asked Scar.

"Yeah. The floor's rotting," Scar replied with a mouth full of food. "What did you expect?"

Drysis picked up her crossbow and stood up, pointing it at the orc fiddle player. He stopped playing.

Shamrok lowered his cards and said, "What's the problem, Drysis? Did a little creak spook you?"

"One can't be too sure." She nodded at Ghost, who crept quietly over to her side.

Dragons of mercy, they are looking right at me.

When Drysis lifted her eye patch, Tanlin moved.

"THEY SAY the waiting is the hardest part," Lythlenion said quietly.

Rhonna, Lythlenion, and Cotton had moved deeper into Daggerford, and in the cover of the buildings, they kept an eye on the tavern Tanlin should have entered.

"I can hear my heart beating in my ears," he continued. He had his back against an alley wall, and his war mace was cradled in his arms. "I should have cast a protection blessing on him. I don't know why I didn't."

"Stop second-guessing yourself. Tanlin knows what he's doing," Rhonna said. She'd extinguished her cigar the moment they entered the town, but her fingertips tingled. Tanlin's time inside the tavern, assuming he was there, was seeming to last forever, and it hadn't been that long.

"Do you folks do this sort of thing often?" Cotton asked.

"More often than we like," Lythlenion said. "I'm a gardener, and she's a blacksmith."

"Oh," Cotton replied. "But you adventure on the side. Make some quick chips? Seize a mystical weapon?"

Rhonna tipped her chin toward the tavern. "I'm here to save my friend from them. No other reason."

"That is good to know. This world is full of foolishness. I hope you will be able to retire in peace... unlike me."

"Listen," Rhonna said, "that youth in there, Dyphestive, he'd never have done what he did. It's not like him. We have to figure it out and hope he's still worth saving."

"I was always taught that everyone is worth saving," Cotton replied as he peered down the road. "But I'm having trouble believing it now. And I'm not a vengeful person. No, not at all. If your friend can be saved, I'd want to see him saved."

"You are a good person, Cotton. I'm so sorry for your loss," Lythlenion said. He moved out of the alley and stood behind Rhonna. "No sign yet?"

"Don't you know that I would have said something? And look at all of those people lingering in the porches and alleys. Something is wrong with them."

"Where the Doom Riders ride, death comes with them," Lythlenion said.

"Why would you say that?" she asked.

"Haven't you heard that?"

"Of course."

"Sorry, Cotton, I shouldn't have said that," Lythlenion said. "Cotton?"

Rhonna turned. There was no sign of the cotton-headed halfling anywhere. "Where did he go?"

They searched the alley and the other side of the street. The halfling had vanished.

"He'll be back," Rhonna said with a wave of her hand. "Where does he have to go?"

"Uh, I think I know where," Lythlenion said. He pointed at the tavern.

Rhonna turned just in time to see Cotton entering the building. "What is that crazy little chipmunk doing?"

"Maybe he was hungry."

The sound of galloping horses caught her ear. She twisted around, grabbed Lythlenion, and pulled him into the alley. The riders were a rugged group of men and women that Rhonna knew all too well. Led by the warrior Sash, the Scourge rode into Daggerford and stopped at the White Salt tavern.

"Horseshoes!" she said. "As if the situation weren't bad enough."

42

Tanlin slid across the floor without making so much as a scuffle. The move carried him out of Drysis's line of sight. On hands and knees, he crawled behind the bar like a scared jackrabbit. Behind him, the floor was washed over with a blue beam of light. He scurried to the back and peeked over the bar.

Drysis's left eye glowed with crystal-blue radiance. It made a cone of light that scanned over the floor like a bull's-eye lantern. *What in Gapoli is that?*

"Search the room," Drysis said to Ghost. Her gaze swept toward the bar.

Tanlin crouched. The blue beam of light reflected off the shelves of bottles above his head,

and the sound of heavy boots on wood started to fall. She was coming his way.

"What are we looking for?" Scar asked. "A squeaky board?" He stepped on a board that groaned. "I think I found one!"

"Silence, fool!" Drysis said.

In his mind, Tanlin could see the cold-blooded woman walking slowly behind the bar. He started to squeeze himself underneath the bar's shelving. *I'm dead. I'm dead. I'm dead.*

He balled up and watched the blue light grow stronger. He saw her foot and her leg, then the rest of her body began to appear behind the bar.

The front doors to the White Salt Tavern creaked on their hinges and slammed into the wall, and someone with a spritely voice said, "Allow me to introduce myself. I am Cotton. You slew my kindred. I demand to know why!"

Drysis's eye beam turned away, and the blue light winked out.

Shamrok let out a hoarse chuckle. "Iron Bones, it looks like you missed one. Go get him! Heh-heh-heh."

Drysis moved away from the bar. "Are you here for vengeance, halfling?"

"No, I am here for an explanation. What sort of people kill innocent people? We're halflings. We did nothing," Cotton said.

Tanlin crawled out of his hiding spot and rose. Cotton was standing in the doorway, facing Drysis and Scar. The halfling appeared even smaller in their commanding presence. He was merely a child next to them. *Cotton, will you get out of here? Run now while you have the chance!*

Drysis pointed her crossbow at the little man's chest. "We don't give explanations."

Cotton balled up his fists. "You will explain it to me! I demand it. You killed women and children. How can such a person do that?" He looked behind her at Dyphestive. "It was him, wasn't it? I saw him killing! I want to speak to him!"

"Oh, this should be intriguing." Scar lifted Cotton by the back of his shirt and held him up like a puppy. He took him over to Dyphestive and set him down on the table. "Go ahead. Talk, you little chipmunk."

"Why did you do it?" the red-faced Cotton demanded. "Why did you do it?"

Dyphestive gave the halfling a stony look.

"Will you get this rodent off my table, Scar? We are playing cards." Shamrok slammed his card on the table. "Well, that hand stank anyway."

"Tell me," Cotton continued. "Why did you kill my Zora? Huh? Why did you kill my precious Zora?"

Tanlin intently watched Dyphestive's stone-cold expression. His eyes didn't widen or show any other sign of surprise.

"And you killed Rhonna," Cotton went on. "Why Rhonna? She was so young. And Tanlin."

If Dyphestive recognized any name that Cotton

mentioned, he didn't show it in the slightest. It sent a chill through him. His brave young friend was gone. *Cotton, get out of there!*

"Are you finished blubbering?" Scar asked as he picked Cotton back up by the shirt collar. He poked his finger at Dyphestive. "He killed the men, and we killed the rest. Does that help?" He drew his dagger. "Now, the question is, who gets to kill you?"

Cotton sobbed. "But there were so few of us. *Why us?*" he howled. "Why us?"

Shamrok plugged his fingers in his ears. "Ettin's Teeth! This one is worse than a shrieking rabbit. Scar, if you don't kill him, I will."

"Go ahead, kill me. I have nothing to live for!" Cotton whined.

"Iron Bones, you finish it," Drysis ordered.

He stood.

Scar handed over the dagger. "Do it so I can get back to eating."

No, Dyphestive. No. With all eyes on Dyphestive, Tanlin placed his hand on a bottle, knowing full well that one aggressive move would reveal his concealment. *I can't let him do this. I can't.*

Dyphestive glanced between the knife and the halfling.

"What are you waiting for?" Scar asked.

Tanlin started to lift the bottle.

Dyphestive's grip tightened on the dagger.

43

Knock. *Knock. Knock.* Sash, the leader of the Scourge, was standing in the doorway. Tanlin couldn't have been more relieved to see Talon's nemesis.

The rugged fighter had short black hair and a wicked grin that oozed self-confidence. He wore black sashes tied around his elbows and knees. "What do we have going on here?"

"An execution, Fish Eyes," Scar said. "What does it look like?"

Sash strutted into the tavern with his arms wide and head moving from side to side. "My kind of party, Razor Face." He eyed Cotton. "So, is that the catch of the day or your dance partner?"

"Watch your tongue," Scar said as he set the halfling down, "or *you'll* be the catch of the day."

Sash wiggled his fingers. "Oo-hoo-hoo."

Tanlin had to admit that even he was impressed with Sash's brazen attitude toward the Doom Riders. Most men wouldn't look them in the eye, but he was fearless. While the rest of the Scourge filed in, he sat down in a chair then tossed his head back toward Drysis and said, "It's good to see you, sister."

"Don't call me that, dog."

The group, which was armed to the teeth, included the attractive Katrina, who wore her green hair in a braided ponytail; Bull, a hulking tower of a warrior with a heavy stare; Hawk, a lean man with the eyes of a predator; Squirrel, a smallish woman with wandering eyes, messy hair, and a fur cloak; and Honzur the wizard, who entered last. He was as bald as an egg, covered in tattoos, and had a nasty scar on his right cheek and many rings on his fingers. He walked with a wooden staff.

Honzur bowed at Drysis's feet and said, "Please, forgive my brother. We pledge our services to Black Frost and honor that same pledge to you, his most prized servant."

"Rise," she said. "Scar, get everyone else out of here."

"What about the halfling?" Scar asked.

"An order is an order," she replied. "Son, what are you waiting for? Finish him."

"Son," Sash said as he leaned back on two chair legs and rolled his thumbs one over the other. "He might have the face of a baby, but he has the body of a Minotaur. When did you make him, Drysis?"

"Your insolence will catch up with you one day, Sash." She eyed Dyphestive. "We are waiting, son."

RHONNA SENT Lythlenion back to camp to fetch the others. "Hurry!"

"What are you going to do?" he asked.

"I'll think of something." She drew her hood over her head. Staying close to the buildings, she hustled down the empty street, ignoring the gawkers that watched her pass.

The Scourge had made it inside only a few moments earlier. She waited by the door, listening to the conversation inside. Drysis's words rattled her bones. She peeked into the building and saw Dyphestive. He'd changed. She could see it in his eyes. *He's going to kill Cotton.*

Without thinking, she stormed into the tavern and said, "Dyphestive! Don't do it!"

Before she could get another word out, Bull picked her up from behind and crushed her in his arms.

Drysis marched over and pulled her hood down. Her eye widened. "Well, I'll be." She lifted a palm. "Iron Bones. Put down the dagger. It seems that we have another visitor. It's my old friend Rhonna. Scar, get everyone else out of here."

"What about the halfling?"

"Leave him with us," she said.

Sash rose from his chair. "Where are the rest of them? We owe them for stealing our dragon."

"Sit down!" Drysis said.

The other patrons were sent fleeing through the front doors, which Scar closed.

"There goes my card game," Shamrok said as he piled up his coins. "But I think I won all of their chips."

"What are you doing here, Rhonna?" Drysis asked.

She looked at Dyphestive. "Looking for him."

Drysis looked Rhonna dead in the eye. "Didn't I warn you not to interfere in my business?"

Rhonna glared back at her. "Yes."

"Then why are you here? Do you have a death wish?"

"I knew that you were up to no good, and I wasn't going to stand around and watch you turn my friend into someone like you."

"Like me? What is wrong with me?" Drysis replied.

"I saw what you did to those halflings. I have no doubt that you've done worse, but I won't let you do that to him." She eyed Dyphestive.

"Iron Bones is exactly who he is meant to be. He is my son. That is all that matters." Drysis gently stroked Rhonna's cheek.

"Get your paw off me. Dyphestive, she's not your mother! She's a liar!"

"This is becoming very interesting," Sash said. "So, if Drysis isn't Baby Face's mother, then who is?"

"Be silent!" Honzur warned him.

"Iron Bones, come over here and meet my old friend Rhonna. And bring your dagger."

TANLIN'S SKIN became clammy as he watched Dyphestive pick up his dagger and walk across the room. Shamrok gave a sinister chuckle. *These people are diabolical.*

Drysis held Rhonna's unhappy face by the chin. "Son, do you know this woman?"

Iron Bones gave a glum response. "No."

"This woman is a threat to your mother and your brothers. She seeks to harm us in many possible ways. You wouldn't like that, would you, my son?"

"No."

"How does that make you feel?" she asked.

"Angry."

"It's not true, Dyphestive. You must listen to me," Rhonna said. "I raised you, back in Havenstock. You must remember. I worked you like a mule."

"Sorry, Rhonna, but he doesn't remember anything of the sort, it seems." Drysis caressed Dyphestive's cheek with the back of her hand. "Do you, my son?"

Sash dropped his hands on his head and said, "Is this what we rode in for? Some twisted family reunion?"

Honzur glared at Sash, who shrugged, pulled up his seat, and sat down.

Tanlin studied the uneasy look on Katrina's face, and she wasn't alone, either. Even Bull and Hawk seemed to show signs of doubt.

"You feel angry, son," Drysis continued. "Angry at this woman that would harm us. That would separate us. What does that make you want to do?"

Dyphestive looked Rhonna dead in the eye and said, "Kill her."

Drysis gave an approving nod and said, "Then do what you must do."

44

"Get the horses! Get the horses!" Lythlenion yelled. He was panting, having sprinted all the way back to camp. His hands were on his knees, and he was still thirty yards away from the campfire. "I can't take another step!"

"Which ones?" Zora asked as she rose from in front of the campfire. Even in the dark she could see Lythlenion's panic-stricken expression.

"Mine—*gasp*—yours!" he said.

In moments, Bowbreaker galloped by Lythlenion with his bow in hand and his hair streaming behind him like a banner.

Zora led two horses toward him and asked, "What happened?"

"What *didn't* happen?" Lythlenion climbed into the

saddle with a groan. "I'll tell you on the way." He snapped the reins. "Yah!"

"Is Tanlin all right?"

"I don't know," he said as he caught his breath. "One moment, we were outside, watching the tavern, and the next, Cotton barged right in there."

"Has he lost his mind?"

"I don't know, but that's not the worst of it," Lythlenion said. "The Scourge showed up!"

"The Scourge? What are *they* doing there?"

"No idea!"

"Where's Rhonna?"

"She stayed behind. I don't know what she's doing. She told me to get you. Where did Bowbreaker go? He doesn't know what is going on! And he hates cities."

"All the more reason to catch up with him before he goes too far." Zora kicked her boots into her horse's ribs. "Yah! Yah!"

TANLIN WATCHED in horror as Dyphestive twisted the dagger in the palm of his hand.

Rhonna, locked in the arms of Bull, looked Dyphestive dead in the eye and said with defiance, "You're going to regret this."

"No," Dyphestive said calmly. "I won't."

With his heart shooting through his throat and his fingers numb, Tanlin lifted the bottle and hurled it at Dyphestive's head. It seemed to travel in slow motion, flying end over end toward the young man's skull. It bonked Dyphestive in the noggin, but he didn't budge an inch. The bottle fell and shattered on the ground.

Tanlin's invisibility remained intact but started to sputter. From out of nowhere, Ghost appeared in front of him, yanked him over the bar, and held him up by the neck.

Desperately trying to get Dyphestive's attention, Tanlin kicked and screamed, "Nooo!"

Dyphestive thrust the dagger home, and Rhonna's eyes went wide.

Drysis's good eye nearly popped out of the socket, and she dropped her crossbow. Her mouth hung open. The dagger was buried hilt deep in her chest.

The distraught Dyphestive screamed in her face, saying, "This is what I must do, Mother!" Dyphestive pushed the dagger deeper and lifted her off the floor. "This is what I must do!"

Drysis flung her arms backward and let out an earsplitting scream of anguish. "Impossible!"

Tanlin blinked. It had all happened so fast. Everyone stared at Drysis. For what seemed like a moment frozen in eternity, no one moved. No one breathed.

The Doom Riders burst into action just as Sash pulled his sword and asked, "What in the nine territories just happened?"

Scar bull-rushed Dyphestive and knocked him to the floor. Shamrok caught Drysis in his arms. The woman's eye was glazed over.

Rhonna thrust the back of her head into Bull's chin, and he dropped her, then she slammed her elbow into his groin. He doubled over. With a twirl of her hammer, she clocked him in the chin and knocked him out cold.

Tanlin tried the same headbutt on Ghost, but it brought stars to his eyes. The Doom Rider slammed him hard to the ground and put a boot on his back. Even with bright spots in his eyes, he had a clear view of everything. Rhonna was squaring off with the Scourge. Dyphestive was wrestling for his life with Scar. The brawl had just begun.

DYPHESTIVE AND SCAR wrought havoc on the tables and chairs in their path. Wood splintered and snapped under their weight.

Scar had murder in his eyes, and Dyphestive's eyes burned with hatred. He wasn't certain what had happed to him until minutes ago, when it all came flooding back. When the old halfling had confronted Dyphestive, accusing him of murdering his family, it had stirred him, and the unsettling feeling came back. But the Doom Riders were his family. They wouldn't betray him. They were one... until Rhonna came.

Her commanding voice cut through the lies and shed light on the truth. Her biting tone rang true. In an instant, he knew what he must do. A voice spoke clearly in his head as he held that dagger. *Kill Drysis.*

Fire and rage stoked the furnace in him, and he slammed Scar through a table. He hated the evil man's guts.

When Scar snaked out his dagger and lunged upward, Dyphestive caught the man's wrist and wrenched it free. "Fight like a man, coward!"

"I'm going to kill you!" Scar said. "By any means." He kicked Dyphestive in the gut, doubling him over, and put him in a headlock. "I'm going to break your neck."

Dyphestive choked, and his eyes bulged.

"Yes! Taste death, Iron Bones, by my hands!" Scar laughed. "You never learned how to fight, anyway!" He cranked up the pressure.

"*Urk!*" As great as Dyphestive's strength was, he couldn't break Scar's hold. His fingers clawed at the veteran fighter's corded arms, and he beat them like hammers, with all that he had. But it wasn't enough.

"What's the matter, boy? Getting weak? Or is it that I'm

so strong?" Scar clenched Dyphestive's thick neck harder. "That's because you are weak, and Scar is supreme!"

Dyphestive's strength ebbed. He clawed at the air, reaching for the bar as his vision faded in and out of blackness.

45

With her hammer in hand and Bull lying at her feet, Rhonna faced the Scourge and said, "So we meet again." She eyed Sash. "Didn't I say if we ever met again, I'd kill you?"

"Yeah, and you're going to wish that you'd killed us last time," Sash replied. "But this time, we have the numbers, and it's you that's going to die."

With the commotion of Dyphestive and Scar battling in the background, she asked calmly, "What makes you think that I'm the only one? You don't think I'd come here alone, do you?"

Katrina and Hawk flanked her. Honzur moved to aid Drysis and started chanting a spell.

"Squirrel, check the door," Sash ordered.

The varmint-faced Squirrel hurried to the door with a

hand crossbow in her grip. She opened it a crack. "Streets are empty," she said in her scratchy voice. "Just a bunch of onlookers cowering on the porches. Now let's turn that dwarf into bacon."

With a loud crash, a table shattered. Scar had Dyphestive in a headlock.

Shamrok was rocking Drysis in his arms. "Don't die. Don't die."

Tanlin's face was planted in the floorboards, and Ghost's boot was on his neck. There was no sign of Cotton.

"Well, you might have the numbers, but you don't have the sense. You're missing something, fools." Rhonna was bluffing, but that was all she had unless Cotton pulled off some sort of miracle. She tapped the head of her hammer in her hand. "Let's have a go at it. The sooner I put you on the floor like this goon behind me, the sooner I can call it a day."

Sasha scratched the back of his neck and said, "Katrina. Hawk. Kill this puffy imp. I'm tired of wasting my breath."

Horseshoes! Rhonna's gaze slid between Katrina and Hawk's longswords. They would both be able to stick her before she could even swing. She turned to stare at Sash, said, "You're mine!" and charged.

DYPHESTIVE'S EYES rolled up into his head until the whites

of his eyes showed. The muscles in his body bulged and heaved. The veins in his neck popped out like snakes. "Nooo!" he choked out. "Get your filthy paw off my neck! Nooo!"

He squatted then thrust up. The move shook Scar, but his iron grip wouldn't break.

"You can't break my grip! No one can!" Scar said. "Victory will be mine! I will break those iron bones!"

On instinct, Dyphestive put some wrestling moves that he had learned into action. He turned his shoulder toward Scar's body. With hand in fist, he rammed his elbow into Scar's gut.

A gust of breath came out of Scar. "Oof!"

Dyphestive hit him again and again, lifting Scar off his feet.

"Nooo!" Scar roared.

"Get!" He hit Scar once more. "Off!" Elbow hit flesh. Bone cracked. "*Me!*" His elbow hit so hard that he broke Scar's grip.

Scar staggered backward, holding his gut. With a snarl on his lips, he spit blood and drew his sword. Hatred burned in his eyes, and he said, "I'm going to kill you."

Dyphestive charged, Scar chopped, and their burly bodies collided. Scar's sword ran through Dyphestive's side. Plowing forward, Dyphestive pushed the man into the wall. The rafters rattled, and the torch brackets shook. The men locked their fingers around one another's necks.

Screaming in one another's faces, they squeezed with all their might.

Scar spit through his teeth, "Die! You will die!"

"Not today!" Dyphestive turned on the pressure.

Scar's neck muscles were as hard as roots. His grip was a mighty vise.

Both men groaned. They teetered back and forth, shuffling over the floor and slamming into the wall. Scar's nose started to bleed. His diamond-hard eyes filled with fear.

Dyphestive had broken him. He could see it in the man's eyes. Scar wilted in Dyphestive's arms, and he loosened his grip.

Then Scar head-butted him in the nose and kicked him in the ribs. Dyphestive fell to the floor.

"Fool!" he said with a hoarse voice as he stood on wobbly legs.

Dyphestive groaned. He was losing blood from the sword in his side. Inching the blade out, he said, "I'm not finished with you yet." He tried to stand and fell back down. His body was weak and his legs wobbly.

"You're finished, boy." Scar pulled his other sword free from his back scabbard. "This time, you're finished."

RHONNA RUSHED Sash with her hammer, and Sash thrust at her chest with his dagger and his sword. She knocked the sword aside, dropped to her knees, and slid toward him. His dagger came down, but her hammer came down faster —right on his foot. *Crack!*

Sash let out a yelp that could be heard across the street. "You little varmint!"

She cocked back for another swing just as the sashes on his elbows and knees came to life like silky slithering snakes. They wrapped themselves around her wrists and ankles in a moment. One of the sashes coiled around her neck. They held her fast on hands and knees.

Scar stood on one foot, and spit flew from his mouth when he said, "It's time to die, you dwarven rodent. I'm going to make a corpse out of you." He aimed his dagger at her chest. "How do you say good riddance in Dwarven?"

46

Red-faced, Rhonna said, "*Luuuuukebehindyou.*"

"Huh?" Sash replied with a head tilt.

The front door of the tavern burst open. Lythlenion, Bowbreaker, and Zora barreled through the gap with a greenish hue emanating from their bodies.

Bowbreaker had his bow tilted sideways with two arrows nocked. He released them, and

Hawk dove right, while Katrina dove left, but they were both hit, and they howled simultaneously.

Sash's head turned. "Squirrel, I told you to keep an eye out!"

"I did!" Squirrel replied. "Or I was." She pointed her hand crossbow at Zora and squeezed the trigger. The bolt zipped toward Zora and ricocheted off her chest.

Zora jump kicked Squirrel in the chest. The older

woman went flying backward with her hands flailing then tripped over a chair and crashed.

Pinning the woman to the ground with a boot to her neck, Zora asked, "Did you miss me?"

Rhonna wrestled against her bindings as she soaked it all in. When she saw Lythlenion charging Sash, she yelled, "Watch it, Lyth! He's quick!"

"Bring it on, orc!" Sash beckoned with his sword. "I'll give you the death you are looking for."

Lythlenion gave a powerful swing of his war mace, Thunderash. Sash parried, and the weapons crashed together in a loud thunderclap. *Krak-boom!*

Sash's sword flew one way, and his body went the other. He skidded across the floor, knocking over chairs and tables.

Rhonna's bindings slipped away from her limbs. She nodded at Lythlenion, who had a triumphant grin on his face. "That's how you do it."

Bowbreaker nocked an arrow. The enemies he'd shot were lying on their chests with arrows in their shoulders. He pulled back the string and scanned the room.

Tanlin cried desperately, "Bowbreaker, watch out!"

He didn't see an enemy, but his senses felt one, and he dropped into a squat.

An invisible blade swished over his head. He executed a leg sweep. The floorboards creaked, and his invisible assailant jumped over it.

Bowbreaker knew who his enemies were. His quick study of the room accounted for all but one, the Doom Rider called Ghost. He closed his eyes. He couldn't trust them, so he would rely on his other heightened senses.

A sword swing whistled through the air, and he dove to one side and rolled up with his back to the wall. Ghost came forward with quiet footsteps. Bowbreaker heard them and loosed his arrow at point-blank range.

With a grunt, Ghost, in his blue mask and dragon armor, appeared. An arrow was lodged in his left shoulder. As if nothing had happened, he advanced, brandishing his sword.

Bowbreaker didn't have time to reload. He jumped away from the first cut, dropped the bow, and locked up Ghost's sword arm.

They shuffled back and forth over the floor. Their backs slammed into the bar, knocking goblets and glasses over, making them shatter on the floor.

Neither Bowbreaker nor Ghost spoke or grunted, and a silent, deadly battle of wills ensued. They locked arms and butted heads. Ghost had the raw strength of an animal. His limbs were as taut as bowstrings, and his joints were as hard as iron. Every move Bowbreaker made, he countered with blocks and new twists.

Ghost slipped his hand out of Bowbreaker's grip and locked it around his throat. Sharp fingernails popped out of his gauntlet and pierced Bowbreaker's neck. Bowbreaker jammed his thumb in the arrow wound of Ghost's shoulders. Both men flexed and trembled.

In a deft move, Ghost snaked a dagger out of his belt and thrust. As quick as a cobra, Bowbreaker caught Ghost's wrist. The tip of the dagger dug into the skin of his belly, but his strong arm forced the dagger back. With the nails digging into his neck, he started to turn the tide. No man alive had ever matched the strength of his string-pulling arm, and no man ever would.

He turned the dagger away from his stomach and thrust into Ghost's belly. Through his sagging skeleton mask, Ghost gave a hushed foul-breathed sigh.

KNEELING ON THE FLOOR, Dyphestive lifted his chin and said to Scar, "Go ahead. Finish it."

"Gladly!" Scar lifted his sword over his head and started to bring it down.

Whop! Scar went flying backward as Lythlenion's war mace connected with his chest, and he rolled across the floor.

Rhonna hooked her arms under Dyphestive's armpits

and lifted. "Get up. We're getting you out of here. Talon! Get out!"

Dyphestive climbed to his feet. On wobbly legs and supported by Rhonna, he limped toward the door. "It's good to see you," he said, panting.

"No time to chat. Get a move on!" she said. "Move, everyone. Move!"

Lythlenion grabbed Dyphestive around the waist. Bowbreaker, Zora, and Tanlin headed toward the doors.

But with minds of their own, the doors slammed shut.

Tanlin and Zora tugged fiercely at the handles.

"They won't budge," she cried.

"Lythlenion, bust those doors open!" Rhonna said.

"Hold him," he said to her. He rushed the door with his war mace, ready to swing.

"No one is going anywhere!" Honzur said loudly.

Dyphestive, Rhonna, Tanlin, Zora, Lythlenion, and Bowbreaker were lifted off their feet by invisible hands. Their arms were pinned to their sides by a powerful force that pressed them together back-to-back.

Though he strained with all of his might, Dyphestive couldn't break the unseen bonds. It was as if a great python had wrapped around him. The wound in his side burned like fire, and the blood loss had sapped his great strength.

Zora gasped. "What has ahold of me? I can't breathe! It hurts."

As Talon slowly spun above the floor, Honzur approached. The rings on his tattooed fingers shone with energy. His close-set, beady eyes were narrowed. He touched his chest and eyeballed Bowbreaker. "You are the one that almost killed me the last time. I'll see to it that you die first. Sash!"

All of the Doom Riders and the Scourge started to recover.

With a grunt, Sash was up and helping his crew to their feet. He stood with Katrina and Hawk, who grimaced. The arrows were still in their backs. Bull finally climbed back up and held his broken jaw. Squirrel picked up her hand crossbow and joined them. Ghost pulled the dagger from his belly like it was nothing more than a thorn. Scar hobbled over, clutching his chest.

Shamrok remained on the floor, holding Drysis in his arms. His face was wet with tears. Her eyes were closed. "Kill them," he muttered. "Kill them all!"

"That is precisely what I intend to do," Honzur said. He extended his hand and curled his fingers toward him. Bowbreaker's levitated body broke away from the revolving pack. "As promised, I'll start with him first. Sash, you know what to do."

The rangy sword fighter gripped his sword and said, "Gladly." He eyed Rhonna. "And I want the dwarf next."

47

lap. Clap. Clap. Clap. Everyone in the tavern looked back at the bar. A person was leaning on the bar, wearing a dark cloak with the hood pulled over his or her head.

"What now?" Sash asked.

Clap. Clap. Clap. Clap.

"Squirrel, shoot him or her," Sash said.

"My pleasure." Squirrel aimed at the clapping person.

With a flick of fingertips, bolts of silvery energy shot from the person's fingers and blew Squirrel's crossbow to pieces. She screamed and wrung her hands, wincing.

"Now that I have your attention," the spell caster said as he lowered his hood and revealed his face, "all I have to say is, did you miss me?"

Dyphestive's eyes grew. His heart leapt for joy. "Grey Cloak!"

"Grey Cloak!" the other members of Talon echoed.

He took a bow. "In the perfect flesh." With silvery fire still dancing on his fingertips, he said, "Now, let the negotiations begin."

"Negotiate?" Sash shrugged. "Negotiate for what, you elven idiot?"

"Simple," Grey Cloak said with flair as he sat on the bar. "My comrades' freedom in exchange for your lives."

The bald-headed Honzur gritted his teeth and said, "This child is bluffing. He is a trickster, nothing more."

"Am I?" Grey Cloak tossed a small lightning bolt from finger to finger. "Or am I a full-fledged Sky Rider?" He glanced upward. "Complete with dragon that is circling above now."

Honzur and Sash looked up at the rafters.

Sash huffed. "There isn't a dragon up there. I'd bet my sword on it. This boy is bluffing. Besides, we have the numbers, lots of numbers."

"Fine, then if you won't believe in what can't be seen, perhaps you will believe in this." Grey Cloak held out the Figurine of Heroes. "Do you remember this, Honzur?"

Honzur pressed his thin black lips together, and he ran his fingers over the jagged scar on his face.

"I can see that you do," Grey Cloak continued. He

hopped off the bar. "It only takes me a whisper to use it before I turn all terror loose."

Talon's members gazed nervously between Sash and Honzur. Dyphestive watched them all, but most of all, he watched his friend, Grey Cloak. No one knew him better than he did. His brother's eyes and jaw had hardened in their months apart. He had changed.

Scar pointed his sword at Grey Cloak and spoke up. "You are the one that we killed. We saw you die."

"No, you failed remarkably, and you're a moment away from failing again."

"The Brothers of Destruction don't fear some adept's bauble," Scar said as Ghost stepped alongside him. "Try us and see."

"I'd be more than happy to oblige now that I have mastered full control of the figurine," Grey Cloak passed his bright-silver hand over it. "Prepare to taste my thunder."

"No! Wait!" Honzur said. "What is your price?"

"Let my comrades go, or face the inevitable consequences."

"None of you will leave here alive!" Scar said.

"Neither will any of you."

"He's full of it!" Scar advanced on Grey Cloak.

Sash cut into the man's path. "Back off, both of you. I've seen what that thing can do. The horror it brings. It killed many of my company."

Scar looked down at Sash and said, "You forget your place. Step aside, or I will end you too."

With his rings aglow, Honzur intervened. "He speaks truth, mighty Doom Rider, even though his unbridled tongue is foolish. We must exercise caution in this matter. If you will, let me handle it. I understand the magic."

"Do as you will, wizard, but if you fail, I'm going to carve up some people, including your men and you," Scar said.

Dyphestive turned his head from left to right as he began to spin in the air. Rhonna and his friends were whispering to each other.

"What is Grey Cloak doing?" Rhonna asked.

"I don't know," Zora said.

"I was talking to Dyphestive."

"I don't have any idea. I haven't seen him in a long time," he said.

"I have a bad feeling about this," Rhonna said.

"Don't say that," Zora replied. "Why would you say that?"

"Because he is a bluffer," Rhonna replied. "And not that good at it."

"I don't think he's bluffing," Lythlenion said.

"Neither do I," Zora said.

"I do," Tanlin added.

Shaking her hands and flicking her singed fingers,

Squirrel walked by and said, "Stifle it. All of you." She glowered at Zora. "Especially you, pretty."

Honzur parted his hands and said, "I'll offer you this. Give me the figurine and the word of power, and I'll let your companions go free."

"No, you won't!" Scar said. "Iron Bones won't leave with anybody but us!"

"Stitch your lips, Scar. Can't you see that he's negotiating?" Sash said.

Scar's bloodshot eyes locked on Sash. "If one of these fools doesn't end you one day, I will."

"Can we all work together on this?" Honzur fixed his eyes on Grey Cloak. "Now, my offer. What do you say?"

Glancing at his friends, Grey Cloak said, "Let all of them go first."

"All but the one called Iron Bones," Scar growled under his breath.

Grey Cloak nodded. "Agreed."

48

———————

"I'm not going anywhere," Rhonna argued. She and Grey Cloak were standing in the doorway. Her cheeks were flushed. "I came to save one of you, and now I'm leaving with neither. That won't happen."

"I'll handle this, Rhonna," Grey Cloak said with a reassuring smile. "I'm a Sky Rider now. I can handle anything." He gently nudged her over the threshold. The others were waiting outside. Sash, Bull, and Squirrel were guarding them.

"Get on your mules and keep riding until we can't see you!" Sash said.

"Quit barking like a dog," Rhonna said. "We're going." She glanced at Grey Cloak. "Don't do anything stupid."

"Me? Never."

Sash left Squirrel outside. "Keep a better eye out this

time." He looked up at the sky. "And watch for dragons." He closed himself and Bull inside.

Bull held his jaw and used his big frame to block any more sudden exits through the door.

"Can we get down to business?" Sash asked.

Grey Cloak and Dyphestive stood in front of Bull, facing all of the others.

Honzur beckoned for the figurine. "We made a deal. Honor it."

"Don't give it to him," Dyphestive said, "but it's good to see you."

"Good to see you too. But a deal is a deal, and remember, I have my dragon." He tossed the figurine to Honzur.

The mage snatched it out of the air.

"Now you only need the word to invoke its power." Grey Cloak produced a small scroll with a golden ribbon tied around it. "Let us go, and you can have it."

Scar marched forward. "This charade has gone on long enough. You can take that scroll and stuff it down your throat for all I care. Black Frost wants that elf. He's coming with me! They both are."

"And I want this artifact, and Black Frost would want it in his service too. It has the power to destroy anything. Perhaps even him."

Scar glowered at the item. "Nothing can destroy Black Frost."

"I can see that you are busy. If you'll open the door,

we'll be more than happy to let you work it out," Grey Cloak said.

"Hand over the scroll," Honzur demanded.

"Don't do it." Dyphestive clutched his wounded side. "You can't trust them." He eyed Scar. "Especially them."

"I have no choice. Honzur, honor your word, or I'll have my dragon wipe out you and this entire place."

"You have a wizard's word."

Grey Cloak tossed the scroll to Sash, who took it to Honzur.

Honzur removed the ribbon and unrolled it. His beady eyes twinkled, and his thin lips moved soundlessly. Nostrils flaring, he said, "This is a true word of power. I can sense it. I commend you."

"Let us go," Grey Cloak demanded.

"Oh, that won't be necessary," Honzur said as he rolled up the scroll. "I have everything I need. Do what you will with them."

As Dyphestive balled up his fists for one last battle, Grey Cloak stuck his hand out. "Wait. I warn you. I am a Sky Rider. I have a dragon."

"Funny. I don't see a dragon," Sash said. "Katrina, do you see a dragon?"

"No," she said as Hawk pulled an arrow out of her back. "I believe you are right. The youth is bluffing."

Grey Cloak winked at Katrina. "I might bluff, but I don't lie about dragons. Streak!"

Streak popped his head out of Grey Cloak's neck hole, making him look like he had two heads. His pink tongue flicked out of his mouth.

"As the saying goes, two heads are better than one. Now, if any one of you so much as moves a muscle, my dragon will turn your skin to flame."

Scar guffawed. "You fool. That's an ugly fledgling. Not even worth cooking."

"The only one that is going to be cooking is you. Streak, let them have it!"

Before anyone could move, Streak spit a stream of yellow smoke that quickly filled the room. Coughing and hacking broke out, tears streaming down people's faces.

Grey Cloak said to Dyphestive, "Brother, I know you're hurting, but get us out of here." He turned him toward the door, where Bull was waiting with watery eyes.

"I still have enough left. Climb on."

Grey Cloak latched onto Dyphestive's back. A stream of nasty dragon smoke continued to spew out of Streak's mouth. The enemies fumbled through the foul mist.

Dyphestive turned toward the door and clawed his boot over the floor like a bull. His nostrils flared. He charged, shouting, "Gangway!"

Bull braced for impact. Dyphestive lowered his shoulder and hit Bull like a mallet striking a spike. He drove Bull's muscular body into the doors, splintering wood, and plowed over a wide-eyed Squirrel.

Crane was in his wagon, eyes wide. "Hurry! Hurry!"

"Who's that?" Dyphestive asked as he leapt off the steps.

"A friend," he replied.

Dyphestive dove into the back of the wagon.

Crane flicked his carriage whip. "Yah, Vixen! Yah!"

The wagon jumped forward and barreled down the street to the wild cries and cheers of the cowardly onlookers.

As smoke billowed out of the tavern, Cotton raced out. He chased after the wagon, waving his hands.

"Stop!" Dyphestive said. "Stop!"

"We can't stop now," Grey Cloak argued. "Who is that?"

"Stop the wagon!" Dyphestive said.

Grey Cloak nodded at Crane.

"I'll slow down, but I'm not stopping," Crane said as he tugged on the reins. "Whoa."

The wagon slowed, and Cotton's little legs pumped as fast as they would take him.

Dyphestive hung out of the back of the wagon, waving him on. "Come on. Come on."

The Doom Riders and the Scourge stumbled out of the tavern, down the steps, and into the street, shouting. They were rubbing their eyes, coughing, and pointing down the street.

Cotton caught up with the wagon and stretched out his tiny hand. Dyphestive hauled him in.

But as soon as he was in, Cotton squirmed out of his hands. "Release me, demon!"

"Are we settled?" Crane asked.

Grey Cloak watched the Doom Riders run to the stables and the Scourge mount their horses. "Go, Crane! Go!"

49

The wagon sped north, with Vixen pulling as fast as she could.

Dyphestive corralled Grey Cloak in his arms and held tight. "I thought I'd never see you again, blood brother!"

Grey Cloak choked and rapidly patted Dyphestive's back. "Easy. You're making my eyes bug out."

Dyphestive loosed his hug.

"That's better. It's good to see you, too, brother."

They broke off the hug and settled into the wagon.

Cotton climbed onto the front bench with Crane and said, "Hello."

Crane nodded. "Hello."

Seeing Dyphestive clutching his bloody side, Grey Cloak asked, "How bad is it?"

"I've had worse. I'll manage," Dyphestive replied. "You

shouldn't have given up the Figurine of Heroes. They'll use it against us."

Grey Cloak smirked. "No, they won't." He pulled the Figurine of Heroes from his inner cloak pocket. "This is the real one. The other was a carving I made. I bluffed that weasel-eyed wizard."

"Ha! I didn't know you could carve."

"The roads have been long, and I picked up a new craft." He tipped his head at the wagon driver. "That's Crane. He taught me. Anyway, I didn't have any ideas what to whittle, so I did the figurine because I'm not that good yet. It was simple. And the blackwood turns as smooth as marble when you polish it. I never thought it would come in handy."

"You always think of something." The wagon bounced so hard Dyphestive almost fell out, and he grimaced when he came back down. He looked at Streak, who still had his head popped out of the hood. "So that's your dragon?"

Grey Cloak patted his dragon's head. "This is Streak. Streak, meet Dyphestive."

Streak flicked his tongue out.

Dyphestive waved his fingers. "What is this talk that you are a Sky Rider? And where'd you learn to use magic?"

The wagon rumbled down the country road, with horse hooves thundering, jostling Grey Cloak as he spoke. "I've been training with the Sky Riders, in part, during our search for you. It's a long story, but, well, I've learned a few things, magic among them. As for Streak, well, he is my dragon. We chose one another."

"He's got a head as flat as a shovel. He's a runt, isn't he?"

"You still know your dragons, but yes."

"Why didn't you pick a big one?"

"Because I learned that I hate flying." He nuzzled Streak's nose. "And I like him better. He makes stinky smoke."

Dyphestive rolled his eyes and looked over his shoulder. "I guess they aren't done with us yet."

The Doom Riders were racing after them on the backs of their fiery-eyed gourn. Scar and Ghost were in the lead. Two riderless gourn were running behind them, with some of the Scourge riding even farther back. They were all closing in.

"Crane, if you don't get this old mare moving, some undesirables are going to join our wagon party!" Grey Cloak said.

At the same time, Crane and Cotton looked behind them.

"Don't you have something to shoot them with?" Cotton asked. "Throw a horseshoe or something!"

"Gourn eat horseshoes," Dyphestive said as he watched the two riderless gourn sprint out in front of the others. Smoke and flames streamed from their mouths and nostrils. "One of them is mine—or *was* mine, but I don't think he'll listen to me now." He put his fingers to his lips and whistled sharply, but the dragon horse didn't stop. "I thought so."

"What did they do to you?" Grey Cloak asked as he eyed his blood brother's armor and gear. He picked up a black leather mask that had fallen into the wagon. "Turn you into one of them?"

Shame-faced, Dyphestive said, "I'm afraid so. I did horrible things when I rode with them." He teared up. "I lost myself."

Grey Cloak felt an invisible hand squeeze his chest. Pain and torment were in Dyphestive's eyes. Guilt assailed Grey Cloak, and he grabbed his brother's knee. "I'm sorry, brother. I tried to find you sooner."

The Doom Riders closed within twenty horse lengths. Dyphestive and Grey Cloak pulled their swords and nodded at one another.

"At least we will go down together," Dyphestive said.

Grey Cloak shook his head. "I'm not going back to Dark Mountain, and you aren't, either." He remembered what Dyphestive had said and grabbed the box of horseshoes. He lifted one, summoned his wizardry, and charged it with silver fire, then he hurled it at the Doom Riders. "Yah!"

The horseshoe spun like a grinding wheel shooting sparks. It hit the noggin of a charging gourn and exploded on impact.

The gourn bucked. Its skull was on fire, but it just shook its mane and charged again.

"Zooks!" Grey Cloak cried as he charged up another horseshoe. "What are those things made of?"

"Hate," Dyphestive said. "Give me a horseshoe. I want to throw one at Scar!"

"You'll burn your hand," Grey Cloak warned.

"I don't care." He snatched the horseshoe out of Grey Cloak's hand, stood up, and threw it. The horseshoe flipped end over end and sailed well above Scar's head and exploded to the side of the road in the woodland.

Shaking his head, Grey Cloak said, "You always *were* a lousy shot. I should have remembered that."

"Throw another one," Dyphestive said.

"Yes, another!" Cotton added.

Grey Cloak picked up another horseshoe. He started to charge it, but the energy in his hand flickered out.

"What happened?" Dyphestive asked.

"I've used all of my wizardry," Grey Cloak said, feeling light-headed. He sank back into the wagon with a grim look on his face. "Sorry, but I'm dried up."

The Doom Riders narrowed the gap.

50

Eyeing the fire coming from the gourn's mouths, Grey Cloak reached for the Figurine of Heroes.

"Riders ahead! We have riders ahead!" Crane shouted.

With the wagon bouncing beneath his feet, Grey Cloak rose. Rhonna, Lythlenion, Bowbreaker, Zora, and Tanlin were ahead of them. "That's Talon." He waved his hands and screamed, "Run! Run! Run!"

Talon launched their horses into a full gallop. The wagon raced behind them.

"Tell them to get in!" Crane said.

"What? In the wagon?" Grey Cloak asked. "It will slow us down!"

"That's not going to make any difference now. Tell them to get in!" Crane ordered.

Dyphestive slung horseshoes at the gourn. Scar and

Ghost caught up to the riderless gourn, and they rode four abreast, flames bursting from all four of the beasts' mouths.

"Stop wasting horseshoes!" Grey Cloak said. "You couldn't hit the side of a barn."

Dyphestive winged another ring through the air. "I'm getting closer." The horseshoe missed Scar and Ghost by a horse length over their heads. "See?"

Grey Cloak waved his friends back.

The Doom Riders, with the Scourge in tow, were only ten horse lengths away.

Talon let the wagon catch up with them and ran alongside it.

Grey Cloak and Crane started shouting, "Get in the wagon! Get in the wagon!"

"Are you out of your skull?" Rhonna asked. "They'll run us down!"

"No, they won't!" Crane beamed. "Trust me!"

"You can trust him," Tanlin said as he looked back at the Doom Riders. "I do." He was riding along the left side of the wagon, and he stretched out his arms for Dyphestive to haul him in. "Rhonna, don't be stubborn. Come on."

"I'm not stubborn! Just stupid, apparently!" She gave a yell as she leapt off her horse and into Dyphestive's arms. "Good catch. And good to see you."

Dyphestive gave her a quick hug.

"Don't get soft on me now," she said as she hugged him back.

On the right side of the wagon, Zora stood on her horse's saddle, holding the reins. "You better catch me, Grey Cloak."

"I'd never let you down!"

She leaped for her life right into his awaiting arms and gave him a kiss on the cheek. "I missed you!"

"You, too," he said.

"Make room for me!" Lythlenion dove into the wagon and rolled flat on his back. "Thanks for breaking my fall."

The Doom Riders were only two horse lengths away. The wagon was slowing.

With the Figurine of Heroes firm in his grip, Grey Cloak said, "Crane, whatever your plan is, do it now!"

Crane's eyes filled with excitement, and with a smile, he said, "Hang on to something, everyone. It's time to get the wagon wheels and the horseshoes burning." He quickly flicked the carriage whip three times, like something was going to happen, but nothing did. His face filled with surprise. "I don't know what's wrong." He flicked the whip again.

"Hurry!" Grey Cloak said.

The Doom Riders were a horse length away, and the dragons were spitting fire at the wagon's back end.

"Hurry!" He was about to mutter the word of power.

Crane flicked the small rod and whip. That time, the tip of the whip caught fire. "There she goes." He cracked the whip on his horse's back. "Ignitus, Vixen!" He leaned over and cracked it at the wheels. "Ignitus, wheels!"

A snake of red fire slithered out of the whip's tail and set Vixen's horseshoes aflame. The wheels caught fire on the second snake of flame.

Vixen's eyes turned bloodred, and smoke streamed out of her mouth. She transformed from an everyday dapple-grey rider to a nightmare steed from the netherworld.

All of a sudden, the wagon lurched ahead, flames roaring from the wheels. It pulled away from the Doom Riders and picked up speed. Everyone started waving at Bowbreaker, beckoning him to come in. He was riding along on Zora's side.

"Get in the wagon!" Zora pleaded.

"No," Bowbreaker said. "I'll lead some of them away. Be well." He peeled off.

Zora begged with outstretched arms, "Bowbreaker, please! Come back!"

But Bowbreaker passed behind them and went off the road and into the forest's blackness.

Ghost went after the elven ranger. Crane turned the wagon off the main road and onto a trail.

"What are you doing?" Tanlin asked as he climbed between Crane and Cotton on the front bench. "I know these roads. This ends in a ravine."

"And you know that Vixen can't run like this forever!"

Crane yelled as he fought with the reins. "And it's a gorge. So hang on."

The wagon rocked from side to side and rattled up a twisting path. The passengers locked arms and held on for dear life. Behind them, the Doom Riders and gourn tried to close the gap again and started to gain ground. The wagon dropped down a hill, and the nightmare Vixen blasted through the low-hanging branches and busted through fallen logs.

Grey Cloak took a peek at the dark pathway. Not so far ahead, it appeared to drop into blackness. "Did you say gorge?" he shouted at Crane.

"Don't worry. Vixen will make the jump!" Crane said.

"How far is it?"

Crane shrugged. "Only a few horse lengths or so." He snapped the reins. "Hang on!"

Vixen thundered down the trail, which bottomed out and sloped up.

Grey Cloak couldn't see the other side of the gap. "Crane, you're crazy!"

"Yeah, I'm as crazy as a cow!"

Vixen rocketed off the edge of the gorge, and every person screamed for dear life. Twin trails of wagon-wheel flames streaked behind them. Horse, wagon, and riders soared through the air, crossing over a black gulf at least twenty horse lengths long. Their wicked pursuers skidded to a halt at the lip of the gorge. Burning hatred built in their darkened eyes.

The wagon crashed down on the other side of the bank and thundered on, leaving a trail of flames and wild cheers behind them.

TALON HAD MADE it to safety. Dyphestive had been rescued, and everyone had survived. They caught their breaths, hugged, and celebrated.

When everyone's emotions had finally settled, Grey Cloak, cradling Streak in his arms, stood among his friends and asked, "What do we do now? Run? Hide?"

"We have to lie low," Tanlin said with a concerned look. "They won't stop searching for us... ever."

"If we need a place to hide, I know the perfect place," Crane suggested with a smile. He raised his eyebrows. "How about a trip to Monarch City?"

Grey Cloak liked the sound of it. "If there are no objections, I say, Monarch City, here we come."

EPILOGUE - DARK MOUNTAIN

In the night, with the surrounding cauldrons burning, Commander Shaw, leader of the Riskers, stood on top of the great temple, facing the greatest dragon that ever lived, Black Frost. He had his dragon helm in one hand and stroked the silver-and-brown hair of his sideburns with two fingers of the other.

"Most Worshipful Black Frost, your forces are gathered," Commander Shaw said. "We are ready to descend on Gunder Island on your command. We will not fail you. The Sky Riders, one and all, will be eradicated from the world."

Black Frost lifted his enormous body into a sitting position. Commander Shaw's neck tilted back. The dragon towered over ten stories tall. Each of his black scales was the size of a knight's shield and shone like burnished armor. His blue eyes burned like great blue flames. His presence was as cold as death.

"No, you won't fail," Black Frost said in a cavernous and cunning voice as he unfolded his coal-black wings. "You won't fail because I am going, too, and Gapoli will never be the same." He launched himself into the sky and let out a roar that shook the mountain. "Beware, Gapoli. The Frost is coming!"

WILL Bowbreaker escape Ghost's pursuit, or will they fight to the death?

How will the blood brothers fare in the marvelous Monarch City?

Will the Sky Riders survive Black Frost's surprise attack or be eliminated once and for all?

PLEASE, leave a review on Iron Bones - Book 4. LINK. They are a huge help!

THE SAGA CONTINUES in Thunder in Gunder: Dragon Wars –

Book 5. On sale now! LINK. Keep turning the page for more exciting details about this series!

ALSO, if you are between books and *want to learn more about who Finster is from the Figurines of Heroes*, you can check him out in my stand-alone sword & sorcery masterpiece:

The Red Citadel and the Sorcerer's Power. On sale now! Link.

AND IF YOU haven't already, signup for my newsletter and grab 3 FREE books including the Dragon Wars Prequel.
WWW.DRAGONWARSBOOKS.COM

TEACHERS AND STUDENTS, if you would like to order paperback copies for you library or classroom, email craig@thedarkslayer.com to receive a special discount.

GEAR UP in this Dragon Wars body armor enchanted with a +2 Coolness factor/+4 at Gaming Conventions. Sizes range from halfling (Small) to Ogre (XXL). LINK . www.society6.com

ABOUT THE AUTHOR

Craig Halloran resides with his family outside his hometown of Charleston, West Virginia. When he isn't entertaining mankind, he is seeking adventure, working out, or watching sports. To learn more about him, go to WWW.DRAGONWARSBOOKS.COM.

*Check me out on Bookbub and follow: HalloranOnBookBub

*I'd love it if you would subscribe to my mailing list: www.craighalloran.com

*On Facebook, you can find me at The Darkslayer Report or Craig Halloran.

*Twitter, Twitter, Twitter. I am there, too: www.twitter.com/CraigHalloran

*And of course, you can always email me at craig@thedarkslayer.com

See my book lists below!

ALSO BY CRAIG HALLORAN

Check out all my great stories...

Free Books

The Darkslayer: Brutal Beginnings

Nath Dragon—Quest for the Thunderstone

Dragon Wars

The Chronicles of Dragon Series 1 (10-book series)

The Hero, the Sword and the Dragons (Book 1)

Dragon Bones and Tombstones (Book 2)

Terror at the Temple (Book 3)

Clutch of the Cleric (Book 4)

Hunt for the Hero (Book 5)

Siege at the Settlements (Book 6)

Strife in the Sky (Book 7)

Fight and the Fury (Book 8)

War in the Winds (Book 9)

Finale (Book 10)

Boxset 1-5

Boxset 6-10

Collector's Edition 1-10

Tail of the Dragon, The Chronicles of Dragon, Series 2 (10-book series)

Tail of the Dragon #1

Claws of the Dragon #2

Battle of the Dragon #3

Eyes of the Dragon #4

Flight of the Dragon #5

Trial of the Dragon #6

Judgement of the Dragon #7

Wrath of the Dragon #8

Power of the Dragon #9

Hour of the Dragon #10

Boxset 1-5

Boxset 6-10

Collector's Edition 1-10

The Odyssey of Nath Dragon Series (New Series) (Prequel to Chronicles of Dragon)

Exiled

Enslaved

Deadly

Hunted

Strife

<u>The Darkslayer Series 1 (6-book series)</u>

Wrath of the Royals (Book 1)

Blades in the Night (Book 2)

Underling Revenge (Book 3)

Danger and the Druid (Book 4)

Outrage in the Outlands (Book 5)

Chaos at the Castle (Book 6)

Boxset 1-3

Boxset 4-6

Omnibus 1-6

<u>The Darkslayer: Bish and Bone, Series 2 (10-book series)</u>

Bish and Bone (Book 1)

Black Blood (Book 2)

Red Death (Book 3)

Lethal Liaisons (Book 4)

Torment and Terror (Book 5)

Brigands and Badlands (Book 6)

War in the Wasteland (Book 7)

Slaughter in the Streets (Book 8)

Hunt of the Beast (Book 9)

The Battle for Bone (Book 10)

Boxset 1-5

Boxset 6-10

Bish and Bone Omnibus (Books 1-10)

CLASH OF HEROES: Nath Dragon meets The Darkslayer mini series

Book 1

Book 2

Book 3

The Henchmen Chronicles

The King's Henchmen

The King's Assassin

The King's Prisoner

The King's Conjurer

The King's Enemies

The King's Spies

The Gamma Earth Cycle

Escape from the Dominion

Flight from the Dominion

Prison of the Dominion

The Supernatural Bounty Hunter Files (10-book series)

Smoke Rising: Book 1

I Smell Smoke: Book 2

Where There's Smoke: Book 3

Smoke on the Water: Book 4

Smoke and Mirrors: Book 5

Up in Smoke: Book 6

Smoke Signals: Book 7

Holy Smoke: Book 8

Smoke Happens: Book 9

Smoke Out: Book 10

Boxset 1-5

Boxset 6-10

Collector's Edition 1-10

Zombie Impact Series

Zombie Day Care: Book 1

Zombie Rehab: Book 2

Zombie Warfare: Book 3

Boxset: Books 1-3

OTHER WORKS & NOVELLAS

The Red Citadel and the Sorcerer's Power